Autumn
Street

LOIS LOWRY

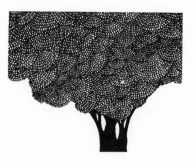

Autumn
Street

Houghton Mifflin Company Boston

For Alix

along the brittle treacherous bright streets
of memory comes my heart
e. e. cummings

Library of Congress Cataloging in Publication Data

Lowry, Lois.
  Autumn street.

  SUMMARY: When her father goes to fight in World War
II, Elizabeth goes with her mother and sister to her
grandfather's house where she learns to face up to the
always puzzling and often cruel realities of the adult
world.
  I. Title.
PZ7.L9673Au   [Fic]   80-376
ISBN 0-395-27812-0

IT WAS A long time ago.

Though it seems, sometimes, that most things that matter happened a long time ago, that is not really true. What is true is this: by the time you realize how much something mattered, time has passed; by the time it stops hurting enough that you can tell about it, first to yourself, and finally to someone else, more time has passed; then, when you sit down to begin the telling, you have to begin this way:

It was a long time ago.

If, instead of a pencil, I held a brush in my hand,
I would paint the scene: the scene of Autumn Street.
Perspective wouldn't matter; it would be distorted
and askew, as it was through my own eyes when I
was six, and Grandfather's house would loom huge,
out of proportion, awesome and austere, with the
clipped lawn as smooth and green as patchwork pockets on a velvet skirt. The rough pink brick of the sidewalk, bordered by elms, would wind the length of
the street, past the Hoffmans' house, past the bright
forsythia bushes that grew around the great-aunts'
front porch, past the homes of strangers and friends
and forgotten people, finally disappearing where the
woods began.

Even today, with a brush, I would blur the woods.
I would blur them with a murky mixture of brown
and green and black, the hueless shade that I know
from my dreams to be the color of pain.

But the sky above Autumn Street would be re-
splendent blue. In the sky, the painted ghosts would
flutter, hovering like Chagall angels, benevolently
smiling down on the strip of Pennsylvania where they
had peopled a year of my life. Grandfather would be
there in the sky, sailing past, holding his cane, wearing his most elegant suit, his tie in place and his hair
impeccably brushed. Grandmother wouldn't sail; she

would hover primly in the most tasteful and protected corner of the heaven, buttoned to her chin and holding her ankles neatly crossed. The great-aunts would soar grandly by, holding hands and tittering, a trio of good manners and barely contained laughter, wearing gauzy dresses that billowed.

Poor little Noah—though I would never have called him that, then—he is among the ghosts, and I would have to paint him lurking somewhere, perhaps behind a cloud, sullen, the only one in my sky who would not be smiling.

Charles. How I would love painting Charles in the bright blue over Autumn Street: feisty and streetwise still, Charles would be shoving and pushing his way across the canvas sky, kicking pebbles, stepping on ants, thrusting the clouds aside and heading for the farthest corner, to explore.

Above them all, majestic, would be Tatie. Tatie would be wearing the reddest, the shiniest of satin dresses, the bright red dress that I promised, when I was six, I would one day give to her. She would be bulky and brown and beautiful, and she would be holding out her arms the way she held them out so often, to me, when I needed a place to hide, a place to cry, a person to hold.

Tatie wouldn't like that. She'd push away my brush, even though it held the red dress she had

dreamed of. "Not me," she'd say, brusquely. "Not
Tatie. I don't want no place in no sky. You paint
in your grandma bigger, Elizabeth. And you paint
in that hat just right on her head, the way she likes
it. Don't you try to be funny with your grandma's
best hat."

I wouldn't be funny with my grandmother's hat.
I'd paint it in carefully, with the tiny black elastic
down behind her ears, holding it neatly to her head,
not a hair out of place.

But for once, for the first time, I'd have my way
with Tatie. With my best brush, with a generous
daub of golden paint, I would paint on Tatie's proud
head a crown that would beat the hell out of Grandmother's black Sunday Episcopal hat.

And then, finally, not yet hovering, but with her
bare feet firmly planted on the lawn of her grandfather's backyard, I would paint a little girl. She
would be looking up. She still lives, and her hair is
still often uncombed; and she still needs, often, a
place to hide, or to cry, or someone to hold. She finds
those things, now, in places far from Autumn Street.
But in the painting she would be back there again.
She would stand there, watching, and would find in
the sky the disparate angels of her childhood. With
one small hand she would wave good-bye.

It was such a long time ago.

"I don't *want* to go to Pennsylvania. I want to stay in New York. Why do we have to live at Grandfather's? Why can't we live at home anymore?"

"Because of the war."

It had been Mama's answer to everything for so long now, that I had learned to accept it as an answer even though I didn't know what "the war" meant. The war had begun when I was four, and when I was four, everything was new, everything was unexpected, so that nothing came, really, as a surprise.

Chicken pox was unexpected, and it itched.

So was poison ivy, and it itched, too.

Kindergarten was new, too, that year, and scary, but Jess, my sister, sat beside me on the bus. She retied both my shoes and my hair ribbons when they came undone. Jessica was a lot like Mama, even though she was only seven.

Then, a surprise called Pearl Harbor. It sounded like a lady's name. At the grocery store on the corner of our New York street, a woman named Pearl sat behind the counter and crocheted.

Daddy had been in the living room that day, reading the paper; Mama was in the kitchen, and the radio was on in the kitchen. I watched her face. Then, frightened, I ran to find Daddy.

"Pearl Harbor is on the radio, Daddy," I told him, "and Mama is crying."

After that, the answer to everything was "Because of the war."

After that, there were air-raid drills at kindergarten. We had to run, holding hands, to the subway station and hide there. Because of the war.

"What're *those?*" I asked, when my mother began to stitch together huge lengths of thick black cloth. I wanted her to make a ruffled dress for my doll.

"Blackout curtains."

"Because of the war?"

"Yes."

"I don't like them."

"No ones does," she said, matter-of-factly, putting blackout curtains into the same category as cod-liver oil: unappealing, necessary, for your own good, and you don't have to like it, but you have to put up with it, preferably without making a face.

There were other things then that I didn't like, and some of them were more clearly defined than the dark enveloping folds that covered our windows because of the war. I didn't like soft-boiled eggs. I didn't like the lady who lived in the upstairs apartment. Sometimes I didn't like Jessica, who said I was too little to play Monopoly with her friends.

When my father explained that maybe he would have to go away to the war, it was just one more thing that I didn't like much. But there were compensations. There was his uniform: deep khaki and glamorously foreign. Sometimes he let me wear the hat while he took my picture. I would march around the New York apartment, wearing pink-flowered pajamas and his major's cap, and he would laugh and tell me I was the best floor show in town. My sister, too sophisticated at seven to provide a floor show, glowered.

Uniforms were nice: my father's especially so, because it was there, available to me, and I could try on the Eisenhower jacket that came to my knees, and people would laugh. But there were other uniforms: the Eagle Scout uniform of my cousin, David, in Michigan, whose parents sent snapshots of him grinning proudly. Then the snapshots changed, and David was in Navy attire, an official photograph, his grin transformed from boyish arrogance to a stranger's smile; and he was no longer the boy I had known summers, who had tickled me gently, buckled my sandals, and allowed me to fall exuberantly in love, for the first time, at the age of three.

Then there were no pictures, only whispers, of David. Whispers between adults. I crept behind chairs, listened, and didn't understand.

"Where's David?" I asked, finally.

They looked at me, startled. It was a question I shouldn't have asked, a question they couldn't answer for someone who was only five. My father was still there, then. I had always thought that Daddy would tell me everything. But when I asked simply, "Where's David?", my father looked away and raised his glass to his mouth, swallowing deeply, holding the ice there against his lips for a long time.

"In San Diego," someone said at last. "In a hospital in San Diego."

I couldn't understand why the answer they gave me seemed to frighten them. It didn't frighten *me*.

Hospitals didn't frighten me; Jessica had gone to a hospital to have her tonsils taken out and they gave her ice cream and toys. Wherever San Diego was, wherever David was, he would be laughing, telling his silly jokes in his slow, soft voice, smoothing someone's hair the way he had once smoothed mine.

But San Diego and the hospital and David all had to do with the war, and so I sighed and left them there, sitting with their drinks and their silence and their fear. I didn't understand the war. It was new, and they all said it would be there for a long time, but where it was, exactly, was one of the things I didn't understand. It seemed to be out-of-doors, and that was why we had the blackout curtains, so that we didn't have to look at it at night—or it didn't have to look at us, perhaps. Yet on some nights we sat on the balcony and watched searchlights play across the dark sky, and that had to do with the war, too. So the war was in the sky, somehow.

And it was there in the daytime, though I was not sure where. It was why sometimes, during school, whistles blew, and we had to run to the subway station. We had to wear dog tags, as my father did; and most children's were made of embossed tin, as my father's were. But mine were gold. Daddy had them made at Tiffany's for me and Jessica, and we wore them on thin gold chains around our necks.

So I had my uniform too. It was not much, a tiny gold tag with my name and address, but it was what I was given to wear as a way of acknowledging the war. It was better than nothing, and it was something to suck on unobtrusively while we sat in the subway station for air-raid drills.

Nothing else that I wore changed when the war came: the polished brown shoes, the knee socks, the plaid skirts that buttoned onto starched white blouses, the hair ribbons that my mother tied each morning into my blonde hair, the dark blue coat with brass buttons, the blue beret that I stuffed into my canvas schoolbag each morning as soon as I was out of my mother's sight. No other child in my kindergarten wore a French beret. There were ways in which I didn't want to be like other children, but wearing a beret was not one of them.

"She refuses to drink her milk at snack time," they wrote home to my parents.

"Why won't you drink your milk at school? You always drink it at home," my mother said.

"It tastes different. I don't like it."

She sighed and wrote a note back requesting that I not have to drink school milk. It was true that it tasted different. The paper container, the straw that collapsed and grew soggy, and the wax that peeled in flakes from the carton all conspired to give a strange papery taste to the warmish milk they placed in front of us at the little kindergarten tables. Even listening to the gurgling sounds that the other children made through their straws as they emptied the containers brought a feeling of gagging to the back of my throat. It was the milk at the very bottom that tasted the worst. By then it was mixed with spit.

At painting, too, I was different. I loved painting, loved the sturdy wooden easels, the thick jars that held the colors, the wide brushes, and the cotton smocks that we wore buttoned down the back. But I could see that my paintings were not the same as the others'. Mine were of landscapes that I had mostly only dreamed or imagined: broad expanses of sky, hills, and mountains, in shades of blue, green, and purple.

I waited carefully for each color to dry before I added the next. The other children didn't wait; they swished their paintbrushes boldly, running the paints together with long drip marks, creating areas that turned brown as the colors flowed into one another. I envied them their boldness, but I loved my beautifully defined hills, my lone trees in their yellow-green meadows. I loved, most of all, the place where the sky and the distant hills met; it was the only part of the paintings where I would allow the colors to run gently together.

It was true, I knew, that in the faraway part of the

countryside where the sky and hills met, the colors were unclear. I had seen it, sometimes, summers in Pennsylvania, had seen how the horizon blurred. I blended those colors carefully with clear water on my thick brush.

"Can you tell me why you paint the sky that way?" a woman asked me in a kind, quiet voice. She was visiting my school.

"What way?" Her question frightened me. I was afraid that I had done it wrong.

"Look how you've painted the sky all the way down to the hills," she pointed out, as if I had done it by chance, as if I had not known. "Now look how the other children have painted the sky."

I looked. The other skies were all blue strips across the top of their papers. I lifted my gold dog tag to my mouth and sucked.

"Yours isn't *wrong*," she said, aware of my anguish. "But it's so different from theirs. Do you know why you do it that way?"

"Because that's the way sky is," I whispered to her. "Sky is all over, not just at the top." But my voice trailed and made it more a question than a conviction.

"Do you have other paintings that you can show me?" she asked.

I took the rolled paintings from my cubbyhole and gave them to her. I watched, terrified, embarrassed, while she spread them out one by one on a table. There were all my skies, all my hills and mountains and fields. I loved those paintings more than anything else at school, more than the cherry-and-whipped-cream dessert that was sometimes served at lunch. But at the same time I had two thoughts that didn't fit together very well: that they were the most beautiful paintings in the world, and that they were, for reasons that I didn't understand, not good enough.

"May I keep some of these? Would you mind?" she asked.

I shook my head shyly. "You can have them all."

She took my paintings away, and I went back to my easel. But the feelings I had about the sky and hills were gone, at least for that day. In a corner of the classroom I could see the visiting woman talk to the teachers; they were glancing at me as they talked. She was pointing to things in my paintings. She was saying something about "Elizabeth's perceptions." Elizabeth was me; but what were perceptions: kinds of mountains or trees? I didn't know, and was humiliated.

I watched as she rolled my perceptions neatly, secured them with rubber bands, and placed them in a briefcase. Her eyes found me, across the room, and she smiled and waved, as if we had a secret together. Then she went away.

"She is a Professor of Education," said our teacher proudly, when the woman was gone. I nodded solemnly, as if I understood.

Finally I picked up my brush again, looked around at the paintings that the other children were making, and tried to do it the way they did. I tried to make a firm, bright blue, bold strip of sky across the top of the paper. But I put too much water on my brush, perhaps on purpose, and the edges of the sky wept slowly down the center of the page.

At home that evening, when my parents told me that now my father, too, would be going away to the war, I asked them to tell me where that meant, and they answered the Pacific. Daddy showed me on a map where the Pacific was. And I could see, even looking at the flat map on the page of a book, that the Pacific must be the place where, even though there were no hills, no mountains, no trees, the sky would be everywhere—not just a thin and hateful strip, but a deep and endless blue that came all the way down, that touched the sea. In that sky the colors would blur, as if you were looking at them through a haze of tears.

"I DON'T LIKE it at Grandfather's," I said sulkily to Mama.

"Why not, Elizabeth?" She buttoned my pajamas and began to brush my hair.

"There are too many rooms. I get lost."

Mama smiled. "That will just take some getting used to. You know, this was my house when I was a little girl, even smaller than you. I used to like all the stairways, and the closets, and porches, and halls. Think of it as a place to explore."

"And Jess won't play with me anymore."

"Well, Jessica is making friends who are her own

age, Liz. You will, too. And you know, when I was little, I didn't have a sister. So I played by myself."

"I'm scared of that boy," I confessed.

Mama looked puzzled. "What boy?"

"In the kitchen. I was in the kitchen talking to Tatie—she lets me lick the bowl when she's making cookies. And there was a boy hiding in the pantry. Tatie made him come out and say hello, but then he ran back in the pantry again and hid, and I could see him looking at me through the crack in the door. Tatie said not to pay any attention to him because he was being rude and no-account."

Mama began to laugh. "That must be Tatie's little grandson. I haven't met him yet, but your grandmother told me that he comes sometimes to visit her. He must be just about your age, Liz. He would be someone you could play with."

"I don't want to play with someone rude and no-account."

"He was just being shy. And what about *you*, Elizabeth Jane Lorimer? If you didn't make an effort to be nice to him, it sounds as if *you* were being rude, too."

"And no-account?"

Mama laughed. "Yes, and no-account, too. Did you say hello to him?"

I shook my head.

"Did you ask him his name?"

I shook my head. "Tatie told me his name. Charles."

Mama patted my hair, put the brush away, and tucked me into bed. "I'm going to go to find Jess and bring her upstairs now. You remember, though, Liz, that you're six years old now. That's big enough to be polite to people. The next time Charles comes to visit Tatie, you try to make him feel welcome. It must be hard for him, visiting here where he doesn't know anyone except Tatie."

"And *she's* only the cook," I said smugly.

Mama frowned. "Elizabeth . . ."

"I know," I said. "That was rude and no-account."

*

"Mama?" I called before she closed the door "When you were a little girl, living here, did you have a pet?"

She thought. "Sometimes. I remember that I had . . ."

"A turtle?"

Mama laughed. "No. I never had a turtle. Why did you ask that?"

I snuggled into my pillow. "I don't know," I said sleepily. "I was just thinking about turtles."

*

Three children in the green, lush-lawned neighborhood where I lived, a stranger in my grandfather's

17

house, had small, moist turtles that they kept in glass bowls from Woolworth's and fed, with their fingers, tiny pieces of limp lettuce. The turtles had American flags hand-painted on their backs, because it was wartime.

Pre-war turtles, I learned, had been decorated with scenic paintings: rainbows, sunsets, and carefully lettered messages from tourist spots. Yosemite. The Grand Canyon. There had been a turtle for every natural wonder of the United States, and all of them had found their way to this small Pennsylvania town, where they had been nurtured in glass bowls, extending their tiny prehistoric heads now and then if you watched long enough.

"They grow to be giant turtles," the doctor's daughter, Anne, told me, as we sat on her back porch and watched her little flag-festooned creature move sluggishly against the sides of his bowl. "They live to be a hundred years old, and by that time they're as big as—oh, as big as the kitchen table!"

I glanced through the screen door and measured her round kitchen table with my eyes, seeing it as a shell, imagining a huge, lizard-like head extending slowly, near the place where the toaster stood. I imagined a thin brown tongue darting from the head, aiming for the kitchen counter, seizing an entire head of lettuce.

I could almost hear the hideous primordial munch. I shuddered.

"Where will you keep him when he gets to be big?" I asked Anne. Her small turtle lurched suddenly from his inverted-dish island and submerged, darkening the colors of his painted American flag.

"He'll escape by then," she said, matter-of-factly. "He'll go out in the woods at the end of Autumn Street, because there's more to eat out there. That's where they all go. There are probably a hundred big turtles out there already. Tommy Price's turtle disappeared three years ago, and someone said they saw it in the woods, eating ferns. They could tell it was his because it said *Mammoth Caves* across its back."

Mammoth Caves. The phrase sent exhilarated, apprehensive chills down my skinny back. A hundred monstrous prehistoric creatures lurking, munching ferns, in the woods at the end of my grandfather's street: and one of them, already grown to ominous proportions, with the words *Mammoth Caves* stretched, elongated, across his mossy, reptilian shell.

I was so terribly frightened of caves, of the whole concept of caves, of dark passages with convoluted turnings, farther and farther into unfathomable blackness, into places where there were no sounds but perhaps a dimly heard dripping, of rock-encrusted walls that wept, and the sound of your own heart beating in a dark much darker, more frightening, than the dark of your worst nightmares. I shivered at the thought that in one place, one dark opening too vast for comprehension, one Mammoth Cave, there would be echoes, that if in the blackness you found the place to stand, on ground that had never been exposed to light or to the experience of human sound, you could call out, and your voice would return to you. From all the passages where you had been, from the place where you stood in the dark so heavy it smothered you, and from the places you had not yet felt your way along, your message would return: thundering from the unfelt walls, disguised and distorted by a higher pitch from a turning far ahead, or eerily in whispers from the tunnels behind. All at once, your own voice: your *voices*, coming at you, murmuring, indistinguishable, in harmonies or discord; and you would have to stand there all alone and listen to the answers that came at you from inside yourself.

I was only six when I knew that about caves and about echoes and knew that I could never go into the woods at the end of Grandfather's street, because in those woods I would have to face the monstrous turtle that prowled, dragging *Mammoth Caves* with him through the ferns and trees, trampling the fragile wildflowers, waiting, probably for me.

"They eat meat, too," said Anne, who was older than I, and who saw nothing in my silence beyond childish interest and admiration. She went into the kitchen, beyond the round table that still, for me, loomed like a scaly-limbed, slow-moving reptile, and took a small bit of hamburger from the refrigerator.

"Probably," she said primly, feeding her small flagged pet from her fingers, "the big ones would eat people."

I fled: fled running down the shaded sidewalk to the safety of my grandfather's house, to the kitchen where Tatie always welcomed me. The brown bulk of her was nothing like the sluggish brown creatures I feared, and I put my arms around her waist, buried my head against her apron, so that she stroked my hair, rubbed my back gently until I was no longer afraid, and then said, "There. Nobody gonna get you. You go wash your face, find Jess, and tell your Mama that dinner be ready soon."

Upstairs, in the big house, Jess was helping our mother fold and put away the intricately embroidered baby clothes, all freshly washed and ironed. Mama was waiting for a baby to be born.

And babies were part of the war, too. Standing in the dim shadows of the wide front hall, outside the parlor, I had heard an elderly, distinguished caller say that during a war baby boys were born. It was nature's way, said the visitor, of creating new males in a world where men were being killed. Stunned, I had heard Grandfather agree.

None of the adults in the parlor that evening had shouted "Unfair!" the way I had shouted it inside myself, silently, standing hidden in the shadows. Who needed babies? It wasn't fair that men, and fathers especially, should go off to places where the war was, to *die* and be gone forever in that blurred and uncertain horizon, so that the people left at home, the mothers and the grandfathers and the little girls, mostly the little girls, ended up with nothing but a baby. And a baby would cry and need to be held and protected. What kind of nature was that, whose way was to take away a father, the one who had always done the holding, the protecting, and replace him with something even smaller and more helpless than oneself?

Nothing was fair, nothing at all.

But no one minded, except me. Mama and Jess smiled, when I found them, showed me the tiny gowns and blankets with their delicate borders of flowers and lace, and told me they would be down for dinner in a minute. I wandered along the upstairs hall, kicking the carpet, into a bathroom to wash my face and hands, and stood on a stool to see myself in the mirror. There were no tear stains on my face, only smudges of healthy Pennsylvania dirt. I had learned to keep my tears inside, most of the time. But my eyes were very large, and very blue; I looked at them for a long time, looking solemnly back at me, and wondered if, when you stood in a place where you were lost and consumed by darkness, it would be safer to keep your eyes open or closed. I blinked, and went down the long staircase to my place at the carefully set table where the silver napkin rings were engraved with initials. Everything was in order there, and brightly lit; the prisms of the crystal chandelier reflected the silver and the light with such intensity that there were not even shadows in the corners. For a moment I felt very safe.

"JESS?"

"What?"

It was always easier, for some reason, to talk to Jessica in the dark. She became maternal in darkness, her voice from the bed beside mine very often gentle and kind, urging me to go to sleep, reassuring me when I woke frightened from a nightmare.

"I don't want Mama to have a baby. Or else I want it to be a girl."

She sighed, the embroidered sheets rustling in the summer night as she turned.

"Don't be silly, Elizabeth. She's already going to

have a baby, and you can't do anything about that. And she wants it to be a boy. Everybody wants it to be a boy. We already *have* two girls."

"If she had a girl, we could name it Felicia," I suggested. I knew that would entice Jess. She named all her dolls Felicia. She wanted her own name to be Felicia, instead of Jessica Kathryn.

She was quiet for a moment, thinking. "Felicia June," she said dreamily. "Because it's going to be born in June," she added, explaining, but I knew her explanation was a lie. The June was for June Allyson. Jess had June Allyson pictures, cut carefully from movie magazines, hidden in her bureau drawer, under the rolled white socks. Jess wasn't allowed to have movie magazines, but the hired girl, Lillian Chestnut, who did the laundry, had hundreds. Lillian Chestnut's own room, above the garage, was filled with movie magazines. Jess and I had once sneaked there on Lillian's day off, had examined all of her belongings, and Jess had stolen the pictures.

"Can't," said Jess suddenly, from her bed, shaking off the fantasy of Felicia June. "It's going to be a boy. All the baby blankets are blue. It's going to be named Gordon James, Junior, for Daddy."

I buried my face in my pillow. I heard my own muffled voice say, "Then Daddy will die."

"What? Take the pillow out of your mouth."

"Daddy will die if it's a boy," I said distinctly.

"What on earth are you talking about? That's preposterous." *Preposterous* was one of Jessica's favorite words.

I told her the secret I had known for several weeks. "It's nature's way. Nature makes boy babies be born when there's a war, and then the men get killed."

"Preposterous," she said again, but her voice was uncertain. "Who told you that?"

"I heard Judge Crandall tell Grandfather," I whimpered. "And Grandfather said 'Yes.'" I burst into tears. "Hold my hand, Jess."

She reached across the gap between our beds, in the darkness, and our hands found each other. Hers felt warm and firm and comforting. But after a second she let mine go, sat up, and said, "Elizabeth! Why is your hand *sticky?*"

"I was licking it." I had been. I had wiped my nose on it, too, but I didn't want to tell her that. "I was wondering what I taste like."

She turned on the light angrily, got out of bed, and went into the bathroom. I could hear her washing her hands. I could hear that she was using soap.

"You're disgusting," she said, when she came back. She arranged her nightgown tidily around her legs, pulled the sheet up, and turned off the light again.

I sighed.

26

"Jess, I could be the boy."

"*What?*" She was still angry at me, about the hand.

"I really want to be a boy. If I could be the boy, then the baby could be a girl."

"You can't do that. You can't change what you are."

"I could. I could wear boys' clothes, and I could cut my hair off. Everyone could call me Gordon."

Jessica took a very long deep breath. "Elizabeth, I want to go to sleep. You *can't* be a boy."

"Why not?"

"Because right now you are six, and when you are six you can wear boys' clothes and look like a boy. But when you are older you are going to get *breasts.*"

I knew that. I had forgotten about it. I didn't like the idea very much.

I reached up under my nightgown with my sticky hand and rubbed my chest. Nothing but ribs. Reassuring. I felt with interest my heartbeat for a while: a soft thu-dump feeling, regular and hypnotic and something no one else knew about but me.

"Good night, Jess," I whispered, but she was already asleep, breathing softly. I realized then, for the first time, that her dreams would always be different from mine.

*

Tap.

Tap.

There were the sounds, in unison, or almost, of the tightly tied shoes, the old ladies' shoes, striking the floor of the back porch as the three great-aunts rocked in their wicker chairs. The whisper of their summer dresses of voile. The murmurs.

There were the sounds of the doves, settling at evening: muted, sad, sleepy calls from one spruce to another.

And the cheerful thwirp of the tree frogs.

Jessica and I moved barefoot through the damp grass at the end of the long yard. I could see her through the twilight, the pale pink of her neatly sashed dress flattened to white as color sank away with the sunset; she stood by the far rosebushes, fastidiously tidying the leaves with her little stick the way we had been shown.

"Nineteen," she called across the yard in her high, clear voice.

How like Jessica to count. We were removing beetles from the leaves of the roses, nudging them with our sticks into cans of kerosene. Jess was orderly, precise. Her hair was combed, her hands were clean, and her beetles, I knew, were probably laid out in businesslike rows at the bottom of the can she carried.

I had dropped mine twice, killing more grass than bugs. Retrieved, my can was slippery and smeared; there was kerosene on my hands and feet, dying beetles lurching back to munch the bushes again, and those in my can were still alive, crawling up the sides to the top. I tried to poke them back down with my stick, and they adhered to the stick, so I scraped them off against the trunk of a maple tree, hoping my great-aunts couldn't see me through the twilight and that the gardener would not find them there in the morning.

They were Japanese beetles, I had been told. I had not been told why the Japanese, who were part of the war in the Pacific, who were out there looking for my father, had loosed insects in my great-aunts' yard. But I scraped at them dutifully with my stick, unproductively, and they dropped off the leaves, not into my can but onto the lawn, so that they could scramble over to the next rosebush for dessert, and every time I scraped one off, the leaf would turn to reveal three more nibbling on the underside.

"Twenty-two," called Jess with satisfaction. "I'm quitting soon. It's too dark."

The can slid through my hands once again, fell to the ground, and it was empty when I picked it up. So I had sealed my father's fate. There was no hope for him at all if I couldn't even fight the Japanese in the backyard of 203 Autumn Street.

"Put the cans in the gardening shed, girls," called Great-aunt Caroline, rising, her white dress now gray in the dusk, against the railing of the porch. "Then wash your hands and I'll give you some lemonade before you go home."

"I got forty-seven," I lied, feeling another Oriental saber enter my father's side with the lie. I put my empty can into the shed, concealed behind some screwdrivers and paintbrushes, and wiped my smeared hands on my skirt.

"Dummy," said Jess with scorn, carefully placing her can and stick on the workbench, in the center, where they could be seen. "You can't even count to forty-seven."

"I can too. One, two, three, four, five . . ."

But she was gone, flitting across the wide lawn in her clean dress, her curls smooth, her fingernails trimmed, her high laugh reaching to the porch where the great-aunts waited to clasp her against soft bosoms scented with lilac cologne and to touch her with their wrinkled, gentle, veined hands.

I caught a firefly as I walked toward the porch, caught it on the first try, after its brief glimmer beside the honeysuckle. I felt it move, saw it flicker in my grimy fist, held my hand to my face and smelled the acrid firefly smell mingled with the thick sweet scent of kerosene. It was mine: I had captured it and made it mine. I would take it, secret in my closed hand, home to Grandfather's house and release it in my room so that its sporadic beacon would soar in the darkness above my dreams.

But when I opened my fingers tentatively to see its light once more, I found it dead. Grief-stricken, I rubbed the broken body—the fragile, lacerated wings—from my sticky hand with the hem of my dress. In the shadows that moved now from the bushes like furry creatures reaching dark paws across the lawn, more fireflies moved and glowed. Frightened by my own failures, I ran from them to the sanctuary of the house.

GRANDMOTHER didn't like me.

She didn't like Jessica, either. She didn't call us Jess and Liz, the way everyone else did. She called us by our full names, snapping out the syllables like the short, even stitches that she put at the edges of her embroidery. Jessica Kathryn. Elizabeth Jane. She said the names as if she were reading them from the label of a bottle filled with bad-tasting medicine.

One dose of Elizabeth Jane before bedtime, I imagined she was thinking as I went to her each evening for her dry-lipped kiss on my cheek. Snap. And the cap was back on the bottle.

"Good night, Elizabeth Jane. Remember to say your prayers."

Then one dose of Jessica Kathryn, which she seemed to find slightly less bitter, perhaps because Jess' cheek was always clean, as mine was not.

Upstairs, undressing together in our big bedroom with the flower-sprigged wallpaper, I asked Jess, "Do you say your prayers?"

She was naked, reaching into the closet for her pink nightgown that hung on a hook beside my blue one. She looked at me in surprise. "Of course I do. I say 'God bless Mama and Daddy and Grandfather and Grandmother and Liz.' When the baby is born I'll say the baby, too."

She stood there for a moment, looking at me, puzzled. Finally she pulled her nightgown over her head. "Don't you?" she asked, as her face emerged.

I was still sitting in the rocking chair trying to untie the knot in my shoe. "No. I never do. I hate prayers."

"*Elizabeth.* Aren't you afraid not to?"

"Afraid of what? Father Thorpe?" The knot came loose, my shoe dropped to the rug, and a generous helping of backyard dirt appeared beside it. " 'Lord Gawd Awlmighty,' " I intoned, standing, imitating Father Thorpe at the Episcopal Church, crossing myself ostentatiously, and then pulled my jersey off over my head.

Jessica giggled nervously. "You sound like Lillian."

Lillian Chestnut had a guitar in her room over the garage. One night Jess and I had crept up the dark stairs, listened outside her bedroom door, and heard her singing "Gawd rides right in the cockpit with me" very slowly, feeling for, and missing, the right chords.

"Prayers don't work," I said, pulling on my night-gown and climbing into bed.

"Liz, aren't you even going to *wash?*" asked Jess, making a face.

I scowled and examined my feet and hands. There were green and brown combinations of grass stains and dirt. I sighed, went into the bathroom, swabbed them halfheartedly with a damp, unsoaped washcloth, rubbed most of the dirt off onto a clean towel, and came back to bed. The covers were up to my chin when Mama came in to kiss us good night. She looked heavy and tired.

"Why doesn't Grandmother like Jess and me?" I asked, after she had kissed us both, hoping to keep her there longer.

"She loves both of you," Mama said.

"But she doesn't *like* us. She doesn't even like *you* a whole lot, and she doesn't like the baby at all, she won't even look at your stomach, she looks the other way all the time."

"Well," Mama sighed, "it's just that she isn't accustomed to having people around. And she's not accustomed to little girls, or to babies."

"But *she* had a little girl, and a baby. Wasn't she nice to you when you were little?"

"Liz, she wasn't my real mother. My real mother died when I was born, and I was all grown up, nineteen years old, when Grandfather married again. So Grandmother hasn't ever had children. That's why it's hard for her to get used to them."

I was stunned. Even Jessica had sat back up in bed, her eyes wide.

"Who took care of you when you were little?"

"Maids."

"Like Lillian Chestnut?"

Mama laughed. "No. Maids were different then. But Tatie was there, when I was a girl. She came to work here when I was just about your age, just about six."

So it was all right. If Tatie was there, it was all right. Tatie was as good as a mother. Sometimes, I thought guiltily, she was even better. I relaxed and stroked Mama's hand as she sat on the side of my bed.

It was Jessica, not I, who realized what the frightening thing was. "Why did your mother die?" she asked.

Mama didn't say anything for a minute. She was thinking. "It was a long time ago, remember. It was thirty-four years ago. And back then, sometimes ladies died when they had babies."

"But not now. Now they don't." I said firmly.

Mama smiled, leaned over, and took a tiny piece of grass from my tangled hair. "No," she said gently. "Now you girls must go to sleep." She turned off the light.

"They don't, do they, Jess?" I asked, when she was gone.

"I don't know," Jess whispered back.

And in the darkness, in the silence, to myself, I said my prayers. I said them to Lord Gawd Awlmighty, in Father Thorpe's voice, so they would be official and make up for all the prayers I had ignored. I said, Lord Gawd Awlmighty, please don't let Mama die when the baby is born, it's okay to let the baby die if you have to, but if the baby doesn't die make it be a girl, or if it has to be a boy then please don't let Daddy die in the war, don't let the Japanese kill Daddy, I tried as hard as I could to kill their beetles but the can was so slippery I kept dropping it, don't let that count, and Gawd bless Jessica and Grandfather and Grandmother, I'm sorry I don't like Grandmother very much it isn't her fault because she never had babies of her own, I'll

36

wash every night and I'll say my prayers every night, Gawd, if you don't let Mama or Daddy die, Amen.

Then I added, And Tatie, Gawd bless Tatie too. Amen again.

Before I fell asleep I realized that I had forgotten to mention the turtles lurking in the woods at the end of Autumn Street. As long as I was saying prayers anyway, I probably should have asked Gawd to do something about the turtles so that they would never eat me. But by then, I thought, he was probably listening to someone else's prayers, and Grandmother had told me often enough: Elizabeth Jane, it is very rude to interrupt.

In the morning Mama was not there; Grandfather had taken her to the hospital during the night. It was Grandmother who checked distractedly to see if our teeth were brushed and our shoes tied; and it was Tatie, in the kitchen, who held me on her lap and rocked me after breakfast as I sucked my thumb and said the long prayer again and again, silently, in my head.

In the middle of the morning, Grandfather came to the kitchen and told us that the baby had been born, that it was a boy, that Mama was fine, and that a telegram had been sent to Daddy out in the Pacific.

"Praise God," murmured Tatie. "Praise the Lord." I wondered briefly if I should correct her pronunciation, but Tatie didn't like to be corrected. Instead, I climbed from her lap and asked her to make me some oatmeal cookies. That night, I forgot all my promises, all my prayers, and went to bed without washing; Grandmother would have scolded me for that, but Grandmother didn't bother coming to our room to say good night.

MAKING FRIENDS WITH Charles wasn't difficult. I stuck my tongue out at him while he peered at me from behind the pantry door. He stuck his tongue out, even farther, in reply. I giggled. He giggled. We stuck our tongues out simultaneously.

"You two no-accounts stop that," ordered Tatie.

"If you gave us each a cookie, we couldn't stick out our tongues," I suggested.

"Yeah," said Charles, poking his head around the door.

We took our cookies to the backyard and talked with our mouths full, spewing crumbs.

"How old are you?" he asked me.

"Six."

"Me too," said Charles. He chewed for a while. "When was you six?" he asked.

"In March. My birthday is the first day of spring."

"Ha," said Charles. "I'm older than you. I'm almost seven."

I chewed for a while. "Can you read?" I asked slyly.

"Course I can't read. I don't go to school till September."

"I can read even though I don't go to school yet," I told him loftily. "My sister showed me how. Every letter has a sound, and if you put the sounds together they make words, and . . ."

But Charles was bored. "I can stand on my head," he said. "Can you stand on your head?"

"No," I admitted. "But your hair is like a pillow. That's probably why you can do it."

"Look, I'll show you." Charles tipped himself upside down on Grandfather's grass and waved his bare brown legs in the air. "Now you try," he said, righting himself.

I tried, and my dress draped itself around my head. Charles roared with laughter, as I fell over into a somersault.

"I see London, I see France, I see Elizabeth's underpants," he chanted.

No one had ever found my underpants particularly interesting before. Jessica's were better—she had some with rosebuds—but mine were ordinary white cotton. I grinned uncertainly at Charles.

"If you pull yours down, I'll pull mine down," Charles suggested.

"Underpants?"

"Yeah," he said.

I shrugged. I didn't mind, though I had a feeling we shouldn't do it in the middle of the yard, with Tatie glancing through the kitchen window now and then. "Out behind the lilacs," I said.

So we did it there, and it was no more interesting than I had anticipated. I watched Mama change the baby's diapers several times a day. Charles was no different, except in color. I seemed something of a disappointment to him, as well, but we were both polite, and thanked each other as we pulled our pants back up. It was a curiously pleasant way to seal a friendship.

Charles had no father. I asked him, after we were friends, if his father had died in the war; but Charles said no, he had just never had no father at all. Later I asked Jess if that were possible, to have no father, ever; she thought it over, and said yes.

"Like baby Gordon," she pointed out. "He's never had a father."

"But he *has* one," I told her. "It's just that Daddy is away at the war."

"But if Daddy didn't come back, ever, then Gordon would never have had a father."

"DON'T SAY THAT."

Jessica shrugged and went back to cutting out her paper dolls. She cut very neatly, on the lines, and kept her sets of paper dolls in a cardboard accordion file, in alphabetical order, with the June Allyson set first.

But Charles had a mother, and his mother was infinitely more interesting than my own. Tatie's only daughter was named Gwendolyn. Sometimes she appeared at Grandfather's house, in the kitchen, and smoked a cigarette, with Tatie opening the windows and fluttering her hands at the smoke so that it would not waft into the realm of Grandmother's nose.

Gwendolyn's fingernails were as long as her Lucky Strikes. Only once had I seen fingernails that long, and it had been in the illustrations of a book of fairy tales, on the hands of a particularly evil witch. But aside from her fingernails, which both frightened and fascinated me, Gwendolyn was not at all like a witch; she had a loud and throaty laugh, long straightened hair, rhinestone jewelry that glittered at her neck and wrists, and clothes that shimmered and rustled.

Charles said that his mother was a secretary. I couldn't imagine how. I pictured her at a typewriter, with her arms lifted high in the air, tapping at the keys with the ends of her nails, a Lucky Strike caught in the corner of her wide, lipsticked mouth.

Grandfather's secretaries at the bank, I knew, because I had been taken there for a visit, were elderly, mirthless, and prim, their white blouses buttoned neatly at the neck and their dark skirts covering their knees.

Gwendolyn sat in the kitchen on a sweltering June day, her legs apart, her shiny skirt pulled high, her toenails polished and exposed in strapped high-heeled sandals. She pulled her blouse loose at the waist and flapped it against her bare brown midriff.

"Gotta ventilate myself," she explained to me, chuckling with her low voice. "Hooie, it's hot. I'm sweatin' in places you wouldn't believe, child."

"Don't you talk to Elizabeth that way," said Tatie disapprovingly.

"She don't mind. You don't mind, do you, child?"

I shook my head solemnly no.

"*I* mind," said Tatie. "What you doing here, Gwendolyn?"

"Came to see if you could keep Charles for the weekend. I'm going to Ocean City. Going to get away from the heat."

"Who you going to Ocean City *with?*"

"Victor."

"You going with Victor, then you ain't going to get away from any heat, Gwendolyn. You taking your heat with you."

Gwendolyn laughed again, her deep back-of-the-throat laugh. "Maybe. Can Charles stay here?"

Tatie sighed. "Charles, you take your things up to my room. You got clean underwear?"

"Yes ma'am." Charles picked up the brown paper bag he had brought and started up the back stairs. I scampered to go with him.

"Not you, Elizabeth. You stay right here."

I pouted. I had never been to Tatie's room. And rooms were important to me; I wanted to know how hers smelled, how it was lighted, where her clothes hung, whether her bed was soft and enveloping, as she was. I daydreamed Tatie's room into being often: I daydreamed it dark and warm, with small lights that glowed gold in the corners. In my mind's picture her dresses hung against a wall like friendly women in a group, their sleeves flowing in slow, shadowed, beckoning gestures with the breeze that came through a small window. It would smell heavy and hot, like the chicken soup she made on Saturdays, with, somehow, the sweet tinge of peach ice cream piercing the warmth. Her bed would be large enough for me to curl beside her, with pillows as huge and yielding as her breasts; there would be a deep crimson blanket as awesome and safe as church, to cover us both.

But the back stairs were forbidden to me. And my own room, shared with my sister at Grandfather's house, was airy and light, cleaned every morning, with ironed sheets on the sturdy pine beds, and no mystery, no cobwebs, the only shadows those of practical and familiar things.

"Charles," I said, as we sat on the ground beside the spruce tree, scribbling designs into the dry dirt with twigs, "have you ever been in the woods at the end of Autumn Street?"

"I don't even know about no woods."

"Yes, you do. At the end of the street, at the dead end, where all those trees are. Have you ever been in there?"

Charles was quiet. "You get there on the sidewalk," he said, finally.

Then I remembered. It was one of the many puzzling rules at Grandfather's house, one of the rules I had questioned, one to which my question had been answered only with the word "Because." "Because why?" drew no answer at all, only a frown. "Because why?" a second time brought banishment to my bedroom.

When Charles came to visit Tatie, he was not allowed to go to the front of the house. Not indoors, or out. He had never seen the library, or the parlor, or my bedroom, or any bedroom except Tatie's. I had shown him the dining room once, and the polished silver arranged in the drawers of the mahogany sideboard, but that had been a secret and private excursion into territory forbidden to Charles. He could play only in the kitchen, the laundry room, the pantry with the flower-arranging sink, the back porch, or the backyard inside the fence. Why? Because. Because why? No one would tell me that.

Charles had never been on the Autumn Street sidewalk that bordered the front of the house. Of course he didn't know about the woods.

"There are giant turtles in the woods," I told him, hoping to share my fear with a friend. "And caves."

"Yeah?" Charles looked interested. He drew a turtle in the earth, a turtle with a small straight tail extending from one end of its oval shell, and a pointed head from the other. Four tiny feet, like table legs. "Where I live," he said ominously, "there's a train goes through."

"I've been on lots of trains," I told him arrogantly. "In New York I rode on trains all the time."

"Not like this one. This one, she's a monster train. She goes through at seven P.M. Hoooie," he said, imitating his mother. "You stand on the track and you get flattened."

46

"Nobody stands on train tracks. That's stupid."

"Look," Charles said. He took from his pocket a flat tarnished disc. "Know what this is?"

I shook my head.

"*Now* it's nuthin'. But usta be it was a dime. I put it on the tracks just before she come through at seven P.M."

He let me hold it. It was flatter, thinner than the gold dog tag that was now in my mother's jewelry box, now that we were in Pennsylvania where there were no air raids. I could see, faintly, the marks that had once identified it as a dime.

"Can I keep it?"

"Nope." Charles took it back, returned it to his pocket. "A guy I know about, he got flattened just like that."

"I don't believe you."

Charles shrugged. "Ask Tatie. His name Willard B. Stanton. He comin' home just before seven P.M., he comin' home *drunk,* and he pass out right on them tracks. Whoooosh. Flatten him right out like that dime. They scrape him right up, fold him into a little box, that's how flattened Willard B. Stanton was."

"Did you *see* him?"

Charles wanted to lie, I could tell. He was tempted. But he said, "No. But everybody talk about it. Ask Tatie."

47

"What's *drunk?*"

Charles shook his head at me in exaggerated disbelief. "What's *drunk?*" he mimicked. "Elizabeth Jane, you so dumb. You the dumbest person I know."

"I can read and you can't."

He ignored that. *"Drunk,"* he explained with the same impatient tolerance that my Sunday School teacher often displayed, "is when you drinks a whole mess of dagowine. Then you acts crazy, then you throws up. Or if you Willard B. Stanton, you gets yourself flattened out straight by a train."

"What's dagowine?"

"Just a thing you drink to get drunk."

"Do you? Does Tatie?" Suddenly I was filled with fear for Tatie, that she might drink dagowine on her day off, lie down on the railroad tracks, and be flattened. I could see in my mind her copious brown body in its starched uniform, as one-dimensional as a paper doll, foldable, inert, immobile, and blank-eyed, gone from me forever.

"Nope. We Full Gospel. Full Gospels don't drink."

"Don't drink dagowine, you mean."

"Right."

He scribbled in the hard earth for a minute. Then he whispered, "I tell you a secret, though. My mama does."

Gwendolyn, with her long, pointed scarlet nails and

48

her laugh like water-fountain bubbles. "Does she get crazy?"

Charles hooted with laughter. "My mama, she crazy all the time. When she drink, she just get crazier. Victor, he fold her right up and bring her home. Him and me, we plunk her into bed. Next morning, she don't remember nuthin'."

"Charles," I said, "your life is more interesting than mine."

"No, it ain't. You got them woods with them turtles. Hey—" he said, thinking, "sometime, when your grandma takin' her nap in the afternoon, you and me could go up the back alley so nobody see us, and . . ."

"No," I said, frightened.

"I ain't scared."

But I was. "No," I told him. "I'm never going into those woods."

Prance, I THOUGHT, liking the word. I am prancing. I am prancing in and out of the kitchen from the back porch, with my feet high in the air like a thoroughbred pony.

In truth, my feet were high because Grandmother, stern and exacting, had braided my pigtails as tightly as she crocheted the edges of organdy placemats; my forehead felt pulled smooth as a mask, and my ears hurt less if I walked on tiptoe. When Mama braided my hair, she did it softly, with deft and accustomed hands.

50

But Mama was busy now, mornings, with the baby.

I wanted to be barefoot, but barefoot was not allowed at Grandfather's house. Going barefoot, said Grandmother, was tasteless and caused hookworm. Often Charles and I shed our shoes beside the garage or out behind the lilac bushes, where no one could see. Before I rebuckled myself into my practical brown sandals, I always checked my feet for small worms that would, I thought, have tiny mouths shaped vaguely like the tops of wire coathangers.

Sometimes Charles and I tasted the dusty Pennsylvania earth that accumulated on our feet. Tatie said that everyone had to eat a peck of dirt before they died. I worried about Charles, because he confessed to me that he had eaten quite a bit already.

"Aren't you afraid of dying?" I asked him.

He sighed his patient, you're-so-dumb-Elizabeth sigh. *"Children* don't die," he pointed out.

Charles was so logical and reassuring. And he was daring. Once he had even tasted a worm.

Sometimes I wondered vaguely if my father had eaten his peck of dirt. Grandmother, I was quite sure, hadn't, and would probably live forever.

"You better not bang that door," Tatie said, as I pranced through again from the porch.

"I'm not," I said haughtily, closing the screen door with exaggerated care. "I never bang the door."

"Ha." She spat on a brown index finger, hissed it against the iron that stood on one end of the ironing board, and unrolled a dampened tablecloth.

I leaned against the tall wooden cupboard that held the kitchen dishes, scratched a smeared-open mosquito bite on one leg with the toe of the opposite sandal, and watched her iron with broad, heavy strokes. Sometimes she let me do the napkins. "You want to see what I did outside? I made a flower store."

She set down the iron with a muted thump and looked at me. "You didn't pick any flowers, did you?"

"Some."

Her hands went to her wide hips and she leaned toward the windows. "You didn't pick them *roses*, did you?" She checked the rose bushes through the window and relaxed.

"Of course not. I'm not *stupid*. I picked hollyhocks. There are three billion hollyhocks out there and nobody likes them anyway and if you turn them upside down they make a lady in an evening dress. Look on the steps. It's not a flower store any more, it's a beauty contest."

She went with me to the back porch and looked patiently at the rows of upside-down hollyhocks, ladies in pink, red, and white gowns, standing on the steps, curling quickly in the sun.

"Be the judge, Tatie. Be the beauty contest judge."

I was prancing again. "Which one should be the win-
ner?"

"Can't pick. They all alike, except for them colors.
Boy, would I like to have me a long red dress."

She and I both looked at her carefully ironed blue
uniform, her starched white apron, and at my tightly
sashed yellow sundress, and chuckled. "Me too," I
said, gathering up the wilting beauty contestants. "I
will, too, someday. So will you. I'll buy you one."

"Ha." She went back into the kitchen, moved the
ironing board to one side, and began preparing lunch.
On the staircase landing in another part of the big
house, a clock chimed twelve times. "Your grandpa
be home soon. Throw away them flowers and you can
help set the table."

"Okay."

"You better not let your grandma hear you say that."

"Say what?"

"Okay."

I shrieked with laughter. "You said it, now! Wait'll
I tell Grandmother *you* said it!"

She swatted my rear, lightly. "You not going to tell
your grandma *nothing* except lunch is ready in a minute. Help me set the table now, and then you can go
ring the bell."

"Wait!" I will, but wait. I want to tell you something. Guess what Grandfather's bringing me. An

autograph book! He promised. He's bringing it today."

She made a face at me. "What kind of book is that? You can't even read good yet."

"It's a book people write in. Your *friends* write in it. Then you have a book with messages from all your friends, just for you. And I can too read good. I can read very, very good."

I tossed my head, wishing for long, thick curls like Jessica's instead of skimpy too-tight braids. Following Tatie into the large, dim dining room, I trailed behind her around the oval table, placing the napkins in their silver rings beside each plate. Then I pranced off to the hall to ring the delicate, hanging chime that signaled lunch.

Grandfather arrived home from the bank, walking, each day at fifteen minutes past twelve. In the summer he wore a white suit and carried an intricately carved cane. Winters, his suits were dark blue and dark gray, and the cane that he carried had an icepick on the tip, to disarm the slippery sidewalks. In February, shortly after we had come to his house to live, I had played with the icepick cane, marred the front steps of the big house, and been reprimanded.

Grandfather sat at one end of the mahogany table at mealtime. Grandmother sat at the other, her tiny imperious feet resting on a cushioned footstool underneath; she would stretch one leg down, pointing her toe, to the buzzer concealed under the Oriental rug, with which she summoned Tatie from the kitchen. My mother sat on Grandmother's left, beside me, her eyes and face in a listening look, always, for sounds from the fretful baby upstairs. Directly opposite me was Jessica, flawless and ringleted. I made hideous faces at her, across the table, under the prismed chandelier, and she ignored me with disdain.

Ritualistic and precise, Grandfather ended lunch each day by rolling his folded napkin into a tube, fitting the tube into the monogrammed ring so that it extended to the same length on either side, commenting graciously on the quality of the meal to Tatie as she removed the plates, and rising from his chair. Somehow, no one except me ever seemed to dirty the napkins; I always folded the soup stains, which were on top of the breakfast egg stains, which were on top of the previous evening's gravy stains, into the center so they wouldn't show. Tatie wrinkled her nose and shook her head at my napkin when she unrolled them all every other day so that Lillian could include them in the laundry.

After lunch, Grandfather always took a ten-minute sitting-up nap in the blue wing chair in the corner of the library. Under no circumstances, not even if the house caught fire or the Japanese appeared with their drawn swords at the front door, was I to interrupt

Grandfather's nap; I was not to bang a door, shout, sing, or thump my feet on the stairs while Grandfather slept after lunch. At one o'clock he would open his eyes, stand, take his carved cane from the place where it rested in the hall closet, and walk back to the bank.

I waited impatiently for him at the front door, caught him as he was going out, and reminded him of the autograph book. Unsurprised, he removed it gravely from his briefcase, glanced through its slippery pastel pages, signed his name solemnly on the first page, and put the book in my hands.

"Look," I told Tatie later, as she wiped the Spode luncheon plates with a linen towel. "Blue, green, yellow, and pink. What color page do you want?"

"Me? I don't want no color. I'm not going to mess up nobody's book."

Sitting perched on a kitchen chair, I giggled at her, and leafed through the pages, feeling the soft leather cover. *My Friends* was the title, embossed diagonally in gold. I had seen the autograph book in the window of the stationery store next to Grandfather's bank, had wheedled gently, and now it was mine.

"Come on, Tatie. What color? Grandfather wrote on a blue page. Look, the very first page. Look what Grandfather wrote. His bank name."

It was his flourished signature, the one I had seen on documents and papers that occasionally lay briefly on the hall table. I hadn't the slightest idea what Grandfather's name was. Although I had been able to read since I was four, I couldn't read his signature, which included initials and was formed with broad, magnificent strokes.

Tatie looked, impressed. "That's real nice. Did your grandma write yet?"

I grimaced. "Yes. On yellow. Listen, though." I sounded the words out carefully, reading Grandmother's message in a Grandmother-like voice: " 'Good manners and good morals are sworn friends and fast allies.' " I clutched my stomach and did my throwing-up imitation. Tatie shrugged.

"Here's Mama's, on the green page. I can read it all right, but I don't understand it. 'I pine fir yew, and sometimes balsam.' Do you know what that means?"

Tatie thought. "No," she said, "but I never could understand your mama too good, not even when she was little."

"Here's Jessica's. It's on green, like Mama's. Listen: 'Too good to be forgotten.' No, wait. You have to look: '2 good 2 B 4 gotten.' Get it? See how the numbers are?"

She leaned over from the sink and glanced at the pale green page. "You know what *I* think," she confided matter-of-factly, "I think Jessica thinks she really *is* too good for some of us."

I giggled again, wondering what Grandmother would say if she heard Tatie talk that way about my sister. "Well," I said, redeeming Jess a little, "her writing is nice and neat, though."

I had to explain something to Tatie, and I was embarrassed. "I can't ask Charles to sign it," I said, finally, "because he can't write yet. After he starts school and learns how to write, then I'm going to give him one of the best pages.

"What color do *you* want, Tatie?" I asked again.

"Told you already. I don't want no color."

"I'm saving one of the blues for Daddy. When he gets home from the war."

"That's right, baby," she said, smiling, remembering my father. "You save the best ones for your daddy."

"Come on, Tatie. Pick a page. I've got to go out and get other people to sign. Pick a page." I dangled the book in front of her. "And don't call me baby," I added.

"Pick a page, pick a page," she mimicked in a high, baby voice, hanging up the dishtowel and ignoring my autograph book. "Not Tatie. Tatie's not picking no page. Now go on outside."

I stood still for a moment, angry at her broad, turned-away back. "Smarty-pants," I said loudly, and stuck out my tongue. She didn't reply, didn't turn around, busied herself silently at the sink, and finally I walked to the screen door. "Smarty smarty smarty," I chanted spitefully and went outside, letting the door bang.

"Ha," I heard her mutter as she scrubbed at the spotless sink.

*

The shades that had been drawn in the library against the early summer heat were raised in the evening, just after dinner, as the sun was setting. Grandfather sat, as always, in the blue wing chair, listening somberly to the seven o'clock news from the big radio in the corner. Grandmother, her feet on a small rush stool, sat upright on one of the summer-slipcovered chairs and stitched at something fragile and elegant. Grandmother's hands seemed never to be still; she stitched, polished, arranged, adjusted, and examined things with precision—and me, sometimes, with distaste.

"Idle hands are the devil's playthings," Grandmother said often. I thought darkly that the devil probably knew more about fun than Grandmother ever would or had; but I sighed in guilt each time she said it, and hid my own idle hands, with their bitten nails, in my pockets or behind my back.

Mama was at the Governor Winthrop desk, writing a letter on pale blue rustling paper. Jessica sat on the rug, her dress tucked neatly around her legs, looking at a *National Geographic;* I wondered idly if she were looking for naked people, the way I did. Upstairs, the wailing baby had finally surrendered to sleep in the small pine crib which had held my half-orphaned mother thirty-four years before.

I read and reread the smudged, cryptic, and sentimental verses in my autograph book.

"Fourteen people signed it today," I announced when the radio news had ended.

"So?" remarked Jess, smoothing her curls. "How many of them were movie stars?" Then she quickly turned her magazine page, avoiding Grandmother's cold glance.

"Would you like me to read you some, Grandfather?" I asked.

"Certainly. Read me a few while I get out the Chinese Checkers," he said obligingly. We always played Chinese Checkers after dinner. Grandfather always had the blue marbles, and Grandfather always won. Again and again he pointed out to Jess and me how we could win if we'd only plan ahead. But we floundered and hesitated. The blue marbles overtook us every time.

"Listen, everyone. This is from Anne. 'I auto cry, I auto laugh, I auto give you my autograph.' It's on a yellow page."

Mama looked up and smiled.

"Here," I said, holding up the book. "You have to see this one. See how the writing goes around in a circle? Listen: 'Remember the girl from the city, remember the girl from the town, remember the girl who spoiled your book by writing upside down.' Nancy Norcross wrote that."

"Did the Norcross girl really spoil your book, Elizabeth?" asked Grandmother, neatly snipping off a thread.

"No, Grandmother. It was just a joke. Here, listen to this one, it's from Mrs. Hoffman: 'Make new friends, but keep the old, one is silver, the other gold.' "

"Yes, that's nice, dear," said Mama, looking back at her unfinished letter.

"May I assume that no one else wants the blue marbles?" asked Grandfather, already arranging them in his point of the star. We all shook our heads.

"Tatie wouldn't sign it," I said, pouting.

Mama looked up again. "Don't bother Tatie with it, Liz. She's too busy."

"What do you want her to sign it for anyway? It's supposed to be your friends," said Jess.

"Come on, come on, the game is starting. Who's red tonight? Who wants to be black?" Grandfather was already examining his blue marbles, planning ahead, plotting his moves.

"She *is* my friend. I want her to sign it on this pink page I'm saving for her. Can you tell her to sign it, Grandfather?"

"What? Tatie? No. No, I can't tell her to do that. She can make her own decisions. Don't pester her with it, though."

Mama sighed and looked up again. "You have plenty of friends. You don't *need* her to sign it."

Grandmother had settled her sewing into a wicker basket and was moving to the Chinese Checkers table. "I'll be the white marbles tonight, I think. She can't write, anyway." She began arranging her starpoint meticulously.

"What do you mean?" I stood up belligerently and faced Grandmother.

"Just what I said, miss. Now take off that frown and arrange your marbles."

"She can too," I said.

And the room was suddenly, startlingly silent. Jessica looked up at me with a kind of fearful admiration. Mama stopped writing, bit her lip, and said nothing. The clock on the staircase landing chimed once. Seven-thirty. I glared at Grandmother.

"Watch your tongue, Elizabeth Jane," she said, through brittle lips. "Tatie cannot write. Nor can she read. She has never been to school. You are not to torment her with that silly book anymore. Now

62

sit down. We are waiting to begin this game."

Jess moved to her place around the star and began arranging the red marbles silently. I watched her for a moment and then turned and left the room.

Tatie was in the kitchen, humming as she put away the silverware. She looked at me, grinned, and said, "You better watch out your face don't freeze that way, you might scare somebody."

I put the autograph book on the table, turned to a blank pink page, and handed her my pencil. "Just write your name," I commanded. "You don't have to write a poem or anything."

But her face went as stony and stubborn as mine. "I told you this afternoon," she said, "I don't care nothing about writing in that book."

I grabbed her hand, still damp from the dishtowel, put the pencil into it, and begged. "Please. Just your name is all. I really need it, Tatie."

She wiped her hands slowly on the white apron of her black evening uniform, watching me. Then she leaned to the book with the pencil, smoothed the page flat, and made the beginning of a mark: a careful, curling line at the side of the pink page, before she put the pencil down. "I can't," she said, with angry, challenging dignity.

"You can *too*," I said defiantly, putting the pencil again into her hand and clasping my own hand around hers. I forced her hand to the page and guided it into a *T,* and then an *A.* "See? I told you you could. You make me so mad, not wanting to write in my book!" I muttered, through clenched teeth, pressing her hand into an unresisting *T,* an *I,* and an *E.* "Now cross the *T*'s."

"What?" She looked at me in bewilderment.

"Cross your *T*'s," I ordered, tears hot behind my eyes. "You always have to cross your *T*'s. Here." And I took her hand once more, more gently, as gently as she had often taken mine, and guided it to the top of the uncrossed *T*'s. She drew the lines herself.

Then she looked at the pink page, at the huge, wavy signature, and chuckled. "Well, that don't look too bad," she said.

"Thank you," I whispered, and ran from the kitchen.

In the library the Chinese Checkers game was proceeding without me, in silence. Grandmother and Jess were carefully tending their marbles in little groupings across the board, and over them, with his blue marbles, Grandfather was jumping in direct, well-plotted lines, toward his win.

I held out the autograph book, open to the pink page. "She can too," I said.

"Sit down," said Grandmother, "and put that book away until your manners improve."

I held the book closer, insolently, in front of her smooth, unrouged, tight-lipped face, and waved it back and forth. "She can too can too can too" I cried over and over, stamping my feet on the thick, muffling carpet. The tears came and fell onto the star-shaped board, onto the marbles; my nose dripped onto my upper lip and I screamed at my grandmother, who sat stiffly immobile, "Say she can! Say it! Say she can!" until my mother rose from the mahogany desk and swiftly, silently, holding me close to her, carried me out of the library and up the long staircase to my bed.

ONE WEEKEND LATE in June, Charles took me into the pantry, behind the door, where Tatie couldn't see us, and showed me that he had a knife. It wasn't much of a knife: rusty, with a chipped blade; and when it was folded into its holder, it was very small. Still, it was both frightening and exciting that Charles had a knife.

"Where did you get it?" I whispered.

"Found it by the railroad tracks," he said.

"Maybe it belonged to Willard B. Stanton."

"Who?"

"The guy you told me about. The one who got flattened by the train."

Charles shook his head at me and rolled his eyes. "Elizabeth, you so dumb. Willard B. Stanton got flattened about twenty years ago. This ain't his knife. Anyway, it don't matter who it belonged to. Because now it belongs to me. This here is *my* knife."

"What're you going to do with it?" Please, God, I was thinking, don't let Charles want to be blood brothers with me. Pulling down our pants was enough. I don't want to cut myself with that knife, not even to be blood brothers with Charles.

"I dunno. We could go up to the woods and stab them turtles."

"No."

"Elizabeth, *some*time we got to go."

"No. Maybe sometime. Not yet."

"Well," said Charles, "we could scare Ferdie Gossett."

"Who?" Why did Charles know about so many things, so many people, that I didn't know about?

"You never seen Ferdie Gossett? That crazy guy who walks around town talking to hisself?"

I shook my head. "I'm not allowed to go away from this block."

Charles sighed, and we both were silent, thinking.

Everything worth stabbing or scaring was too far from Grandfather's house.

Except Noah Hoffman.

"Charles," I whispered, "we could scare Noah Hoffman."

Charles brightened. I was scared, myself, for having thought of it, but pleased that the idea appealed to Charles.

"Yeah," he said. "First we scare him. Then we *stab* him."

I cringed. "Not stab him, Charles. Not *kill* him."

"I didn't mean kill him, stupid. Just stab him a little bitty ole wound. Maybe in his leg or something. Remember what he done to that cat?"

I shuddered. A little bitty ole wound would serve Noah Hoffman right. Charles and I had watched him when he killed the cat. We had done nothing, had not known what to do.

"You and me, Charles," I said guiltily, "we're really no-account."

"Yeah," grinned Charles, putting the knife into his pocket. "But Noah Hoffman, he's the no-accountest of all. Let's go look crost the hedge and see what he's doing."

*

Noah and Nathaniel Hoffman, who lived in the house next door to Grandfather's, were twins. They were the only twins I had ever known, and the circumstances of their birth intrigued me in the strange, secret way that birth intrigues all children. "They grew together in their mother's stomach," my own mother had told me, when I had asked how two brothers could both be seven years old at once and why they looked so alike. It had been before my brother's birth; Mama's stomach at the time was so overwhelmingly large with what she assured me was only *one* baby that I didn't see how it could be possible to have two at once. And Mrs. Hoffman was smaller than Mama had ever been: a tiny, thin woman with the nervous mannerisms of a bird. I looked at her stomach, flat behind her flowered housedress, and pictured Noah and Nathaniel both inside like a wooden key-ring puzzle I had once had: entwined, interlocked, separated by someone who knew the secret.

As was true of Jess and me, and Charles, there was no father at the Hoffmans' house. There had been one, once. But he had not gone to the war. He had simply disappeared, sometime during the night, while Mrs. Hoffman and the twins were sleeping. Nathaniel told Charles and me that one afternoon when he visited us shyly in Grandfather's yard.

"Our daddy just went away," he said, "and we didn't ever see him again. He left a note."

Later, from the hallway's shadows where I frequently hid and listened to grownup conversation, I heard Mama discuss the Hoffmans with my grandparents.

"I was talking to Margaret Hoffman today," Mama said, "and she told me that she's taking one of the twins to a psychiatrist in Harrisburg."

Grandmother sniffed. I didn't know what a psychiatrist was, but Grandmother's sniff indicated that it was something tasteless, something in the same category as Baptists, comic books, or lipstick.

"And the psychiatrist told her," Mama went on, "that the reason Noah is having so many problems is partly because of being a twin, and partly because of the father leaving."

"Hugo Hoffman was German," said Grandmother meaningfully.

"Yes, well, that may be. But it must be very difficult for a little boy to have an identical twin brother, and no other male relatives around."

"The father simply disappeared, at the beginning of the war," said Grandmother. "He was German."

"I believe he was second generation," said Grandfather quietly from the blue wing chair, "and that there was, ah, another woman involved."

"German is German," said Grandmother. And sniffed again.

I told Jessica later what I had heard Mama say. She raised her eyebrows briefly. "I'm not going to play with them anyway," Jess said. "I don't like boys. And especially I don't like Noah."

"Are you scared of him?"

"A seven-year-old? Of course not. I just don't like him."

I was afraid of Noah. So was Charles, though he said he wasn't. But Charles and I had watched Noah kill the cat.

Noah and Nathaniel looked spookily alike: tall for their age, thin, and blond. But it was easy to tell them apart. Noah never looked at you. His eyes darted back and forth. And he was never still. He moved constantly, tapping his feet, fluttering his fingers. He fell, and never cried; he broke things, and didn't care. He caused bad things to happen.

I had been in their yard one day in the spring when Noah smashed a rotten log with his fist. It crumbled, revealing swarms of lethargic yellow jackets. Dislodged, they began to hum and move. Some flew toward Noah and attached themselves to his jacket and pants. He ran to the back porch, and called his mother, and Mrs. Hoffman quickly pulled off his clothes and took him inside.

But he was unstung. I could hear through the open window that he was playing in his room.

And on the porch, slowly, the yellow jackets came out of his discarded clothes. Nathaniel had been sitting there all along, by the wicker chairs, playing quietly with a train he had made from oatmeal boxes; suddenly he looked up, startled, and began to cry. The bees were on his face.

The next day Noah announced, in an odd, triumphant fashion, "Look at my brother." Nathaniel's eyes were swollen closed, and he looked like the stretched face on a squeezed balloon. Even distorted as he was, he still looked gentle and puzzled, as always, while Noah taunted and jeered.

Later, when it was warmer and we could leave our jackets at home, I saw Nathaniel's scar for the first time. It was like a vaccination on his lower arm: perfectly round, deep pink, and formed of concentric circles, smaller and smaller until the center of the scar was just a pink dot.

"Noah did it," Nathaniel told me, in his soft, questioning voice, when I asked what it was. "He held the cigarette lighter from the car on my arm."

So there was good reason to be frightened of Noah, even before he killed the cat.

I didn't go through the hedge into their yard any more by late spring. Nathaniel's scar scared me; but more than that, Noah had begun to seem more and more malevolent as the weather became warmer. If he saw me at the hedge, where I sometimes stood, lonely in Grandfather's yard, he lunged at me without warning, using his mother's clothespole as a lance. Behind him, Mrs. Hoffman's wash would fall and drag ignobly on the hard brown grass.

But Charles and I were accomplished at hiding. We watched the Hoffman boys often from hidden places in the hedge or along the fence. We saw Noah one evening after supper, alone in his yard, tease the cat, Pixie, until she playfully leapt into his lap. Then we watched as he carefully twisted her neck with his small hands until she was limp. He left her there by his wagon when his mother called him in for his bath.

We never told anyone. In the morning, when Nathaniel called solemnly through the hedge to me, "Pixie is dead," I called back words of sympathy and felt hate form in a hard knot beside fear. Later Jess, Charles, and I went into Hoffman's yard to attend the funeral of the cat. Noah had dug the grave with his shovel. We all stood at attention while he lowered Pixie in her shoebox casket, covered the grave with earth, and planted a little American flag on the top. Nathaniel held Jess' hand tightly and wept.

So when Charles found the knife and suggested a little bitty ole wound for Noah Hoffman, it seemed profoundly just to us both. We stood on Grandfather's back porch and watched over the hedge. But the Hoffmans' house was unusually still.

We played in Grandfather's yard all afternoon. Beside the garage we carefully cut a worm in half with the knife. If you cut a worm in half, Charles told me, each half would grow into a whole worm. Ours didn't, though we waited, watching it, for quite a long time. Maybe, we decided, it could only do it underground; so we each buried half a worm.

Then we built, in the dirt, a racecourse for ants. We each got a cookie from Tatie, scattered cookie crumbs around the dusty oval of our racetrack, and we knelt and munched chocolate chip cookies and watched ants industriously dealing with the crumbs. The sun was fiercely hot. Above the tin roof of the Hoffmans' garage, when we looked through the hedge to their yard, the air seemed to shimmer and move.

Finally one of the twins came out of the house, carrying a comic book, and sat down on the steps of his back porch.

Charles fingered his pocket where the knife was. "That him?" he asked me. "That Noah?"

I looked carefully. The twins' short-trimmed haircuts were identical. They each had freckles across their cheeks. But the boy on the steps was sitting still, only his mouth moving silently as he sounded out words to himself, reading the newest Captain Marvel. His fingers weren't fluttering. His feet were motionless.

"No," I said. "That's Nathaniel."

Charles sighed. We waited. But Noah did not appear. Nathaniel came to the end of his comic and read the Charles Atlas advertisement on the back cover.

"Hi, Nathaniel," I called finally, through the hedge.

He looked up and smiled. "Hi," he called back. "Noah's sick!"

"Oh."

"He has a temperature of a hundred and four."

"Oh."

"It went almost to the top of the thermometer," Nathaniel said in an awed voice. "The doctor came last night."

It was almost startling to hear Nathaniel talk. When Noah was with him in the yard, Nathaniel barely spoke at all.

"You want to come over and play?" he called.

"Can Charles come?"

"Yeah, bring Charles. You can help me feed the ducks."

The ducks! Charles and I looked at each other with delight.

The Hoffman twins had been given baby ducks for Easter. My envy had reached heights almost to the point of physical pain when I had stood on the back porch, looked over the hedge, and seen the two tinted ducks—pink and green—waddling in the grass.

"Outrageous," Grandmother had said, when she saw them. I had nodded mutely. But when Grandmother went inside, I stayed on the porch and watched; and I wanted a bright-colored duck who would follow me, quacking jauntily, with all my heart. I wanted a little duck more than I wanted a kitten, which had already been refused me; certainly more than I wanted a turtle, which would grow massive and flee to lurk in the woods, hungry for flesh; and I would even, given the opportunity, have traded my mother's then-unborn baby for a small, fluffy, garishly dyed creature that would walk on little webbed feet like a wind-up toy, the way the Hoffmans' ducklings did.

The twins named them Donald and Daisy. They set up an old canvas wading pool, and the ducks floated forlornly on top of the shallow water from the garden hose. They grew larger, louder, more demanding, and less attractive. Their dyed feathers grew out, and were streaked at the ends with pink and green; closer to their bodies, they were thick and white: real duck feathers. I thought them beautiful. I thought their loyalty, as they waddled behind the twins in squat postures of devotion, a heroic, humbling thing.

But my heart went out to Donald Duck. Donald was Noah's; and my heart went out to him from behind the hedge in throbs of sorrow and despair. Noah had devised a game. He had wanted, from the beginning, to leash Donald, and had tried an old dog collar and leash, but the duck's head was too small. Donald slipped loose from any device that Noah concocted. Noah kicked him, sometimes, in anger and frustration, the way I had often seen him kick Pixie. But Donald was stupid, dependent, and humbly submissive; he refused the collar but followed Noah still, walking flat-footedly behind him around the Hoffmans' yard. A leash on a duck that loyal, it seemed to me, was unnecessary. But Noah kept trying.

Finally he found a bizarre method that worked. He discovered that if he fed Donald something of which he was particularly fond, like rye bread, and tied a thread around the bread first, Donald would swallow the thread as well. Then Noah, triumphantly holding the other end of the thread, would lead Donald, gagging and choking, around the yard, dragging him faster and faster as the duck tried, on his short legs and clumsy webbed feet, to keep up. Eventually the thread would break. Then Noah would begin tying up the next piece of rye bread.

Nathaniel timidly pleaded with him to stop. He tried to bribe him with promises of new, unread, unrumpled comic books. For my part, behind the unwieldy and protective hedge, I tried prayer. I cried, silently, watching poor Donald fluttering frantically at the end of the taut, diabolical leash. But Noah continued the game. It made him laugh.

And now Noah was sick, and Charles and I were invited into the Hoffmans' yard to help feed the ducks. Maybe, I thought, pushing through the hedge happily, prayer works after all.

Donald waddled into my lap as I sat on the ground, and I fed him little pieces of bread to which I had attached no threaded traps; and he fluttered and settled down and peed warm onto my leg. I felt the stubby grass under me and the sunshine on my face, and I was blissful, knowing that Noah was upstairs with a temperature of a hundred and four.

"When you think Noah gonna get better?" asked Charles, patting the pink-and-white back of Daisy gingerly. I knew he was thinking of the little knife in his pocket. But the knife didn't matter to me now. I prayed silently that Noah would not get well. Not yet, anyway.

Nathaniel shrugged. "I don't know. Maybe tomorrow."

Charles looked gloomy. He had to go home that evening.

The next day, Noah was worse. I went alone into the Hoffmans' yard where Nathaniel was sitting again on the porch steps.

"His temperature is a hundred and six," Nathaniel

said, with a kind of wonder. "The doctor came again. Noah sees things that aren't there—faces on the ceiling—and my mother had to stay up all night, rubbing him with alcohol."

"He has pneumonia," Nathaniel added.

"Noah pneumonia," I repeated dreamily, liking the sound. "Noah pneumonia."

We got the ducks out of their pen, sat on the grass, and stroked the mottled feathered backs. "Which one do you think can swim faster?" I asked.

"Daisy," said Nathaniel with satisfaction.

"I bet Donald can," I said. I was already thinking of Donald as mine. "You want to have a duck race?"

Mrs. Hoffman appeared on the back porch. She looked tense, tired, and distracted. "Noah's asleep," she said to us. "I have to go to the drugstore to get some more medicine. Is your mother home, Elizabeth?"

"Yes. She's feeding the baby."

She stood there indecisively, holding some prescriptions in her hand. Finally she said, "I'll only be gone about fifteen minutes. If you children hear Noah wake up"—she looked up toward his bedroom window, open to the sunshine—"would you go up and give him some sips of ginger ale?"

Nathaniel and I nodded.

"Don't let him cry."

We nodded again. It seemed a crazy injunction,

79

not to let Noah cry. Noah never cried. He made Nathaniel cry. He had made *me* cry. But Noah never cried.

"I'll be right back," she said, and disappeared.

"Let's have a duck race across the wading pool," I said, after she had gone.

We put the ducks in one at a time, again and again, holding bread to them from the opposite side of the pool and timing their brief swims. The timing was erratic; we had no stopwatch, not even an ordinary wristwatch. We called out numbers from one to ten as they swam. Each of us cheated, speeding the count for our own duck.

Upstairs, Noah began to cry. We could hear the sound through the open window, through the heat-laden air of the yard.

I concentrated on the duck race, whispering instructions to Donald—*my* duck, Donald—as he quacked restlessly beside me, waiting for his turn. It occurred to me in some corner of my consciousness that the crying did not sound like Noah.

Noah's voice had always been deep, uncommonly so for a small boy. Now, his cry was a high, fearful wail, ending in sobs before it took itself upward again to that curious high pitch unlike his voice. It was mingled with unintelligible words: choked, wet, and panicky, that came at the end of the sobs. It was a sequence, a litany: wail, sob, words, and then the wail again.

"Noah's crying," said Nathaniel nervously. He put his duck, out of turn, into the pool, and began to count loudly, "ONE TWO THREE FOUR FIVE" as the pink-splotched creature swam to the opposite side.

"Watch mine," I insisted, and thrust my duck into the water. "ONE TWO THREE . . ."

We put our ducks in out of order, forgetting, ignoring all the rules we had made, put them both in together, tearing off scraps of bread, racing back and forth between the low sides of the pool, capturing the ducks, flinging them back in, counting, counting, so that we were reciting the numbers together, louder and louder; and it didn't matter who won, who lost, as long as we didn't hear the sound that came from the window of Noah's room.

It's not *my* brother, I found myself thinking.

And: I hate Noah anyway.

In the end, Nathaniel and I lay laughing, exhausted from the frenzied counting, on the damp grass, with the ducks fluttering their feathers fastidiously to dry them, and we declared them both winners; and upstairs the crying had stopped.

It was the next day that Noah died. By then he

was in the hospital, taken there during the night. Frightened, I hid in the shadows of Grandfather's house and listened to the grownups talking.

"The doctor told Margaret Hoffman that nothing could have saved him, he knew that from the night he was delirious and saw the faces on the ceiling," my mother said in a low voice to my grandparents.

"A tragedy," said Grandfather from the blue wing chair.

"Dreadful," said Grandmother. "But we must remember, too, that he was a dreadful child."

Yes, I thought. Noah was a dreadful child. But I was filled with dread myself.

*

"What happens," I asked nonchalantly at dinner, as Tatie was removing the soup bowls before she served the roast veal, "if you do something very bad and don't ever get caught?" Nervously I reached down with one hand, pulled a scab painfully from my knee, and dropped it to the rug.

No one answered me.

"You'll have to be more explicit, Elizabeth," said Grandfather finally. "We don't know what you mean."

"Well, sometimes there are bad things that people do, but they're not against the law, so they don't have to go to jail. Sometimes nobody even knows that they have done it." By now I was sorry that I had brought the subject up.

"In that case," said my mother, "I think the best thing to do is to go and tell the person they've done it *to* that they're sorry."

"What if the person isn't around?" I rubbed my thumb in the bloody spot on my knee. "I mean, maybe the person might even be dead, or something."

That put the whole question into Grandmother's realm. Grandmother was High Church.

"Then the person should go to Confession. Making one's Holy Confession to the Lord, and asking forgiveness, is the only thing to do under those circumstances." Grandmother nodded to Tatie, who stood in the doorway with the platter of veal, and Tatie began to move around the table, serving each of us from the left.

"And if you don't do *that,* then you go to Hell and burn forever," said Jessica with satisfaction, lifting a piece of veal with her fork and grinning across the table at me as the steam rose from it.

"I don't believe that," I muttered.

"Shhh," said Mama, warning me. She changed the subject.

That night I went upstairs before Jess and knelt beside my bed, my grass-stained knees firmly on the thick hooked rug. I folded my hands. By now my

father's face was a blur in my memory, but his forgiving hugs were still more comforting to me than
those I had never experienced from Father Thorpe's
Episcopalian Gawd. So I began, "Our Father,"
stopped, re-began, "My Father," and made my confession to a deity whom I pictured wearing a major's cap,
and who, I remembered vaguely, had once put a dab of
shaving cream on the tip of my nose.

"Please forgive me," I whispered, "because I didn't
mean to, but it was partly me that killed Noah Hoffman."

"What on *earth* are you doing, Liz?" asked Jess,
opening the bedroom door suddenly.

"Looking for a worm. I had it in my pocket and it
fell out onto the rug." Hastily I whispered, under
my breath, "Amen," and went to bed puzzled, frightened, and absolved.

*

Mama and my grandparents went to Noah's funeral. While they were gone, Charles and I wandered out to the backyard and held a funeral of our
own, behind the lilacs. We buried the knife. Neither
of us said very much.

Then we went back to the kitchen, into the pantry,
and washed our hands.

"You two sick?" asked Tatie suspiciously.

My stomach lurched. In my mind, in my memory,

I could hear Nathaniel's little voice call, "Noah's sick!"

"No," said Charles, "we jest wanna eat ice. It's hot out."

Tatie chipped some ice and gave us each a chunk. "Don't you drip on the floor now, you hear?" she said.

"Come on, Charles, let's take it outside."

We sat beside each other on the back steps and sucked ice. The day was muggy and oppressive and still.

"Charles," I said, finally, "you told me that children don't die."

He stood up and threw his ice angrily into the hollyhocks. "So?" he said defiantly. "It was a lie. Maybe I tole you *lots* of lies, Elizabeth!"

He turned his back on me, ran across the yard, and disappeared behind the garage. I sat alone for a while on the steps, holding the ice against my teeth until they ached. Finally I followed him and found him sitting in the dirt, disconsolately arranging pebbles in patterns.

"I can show you how to make letters if you want," I said.

"Okay."

I made an *A* from the pebbles.

"That's an *A*. It's the first letter of the alphabet."

"Yeah, I know the alphabet all the way through."

I rearranged the pebbles. "That's a *B*."

"Yeah."

"Charles, *did* you?"

"Did I *what?*"

"Tell me lots of lies."

Charles picked up the pebbles of the *B* and threw them against the side of the garage. Small puffs of dust rose as they fell to the dirt. "No," he said, not looking at me. "Only jest that one, and it wasn't really a lie. It was because I didn't know."

"OH, JESS," I groaned, "I wish I could be a boy."

Jessica looked over at me quizzically. We were sitting on the shaded side porch, the green slatted blinds pulled partway down against the sun. We each had an embroidery hoop, linen stretched tightly across the circular center. Grandmother had been teaching us both to embroider. It seemed the most boring thing I had ever done.

"What's the matter now?" asked Jess, working her needle neatly through her piece of linen.

"*Look,*" I said glumly, and showed her mine.

Jessica giggled. "Why do you do it crooked?" she asked.

"I can't help it! The needle just goes crooked when I try to do it. And look: those are bloodstains. I keep jabbing myself.

"I wish I could be Charles," I muttered gloomily.

Jess wrinkled her nose. "*Charles!* Why on earth would you want to be Charles?"

I put my embroidery down, put a cushion from the wicker chair over it so that I wouldn't have to look at it, and watched a tiny spider move slowly up and down a nearly invisible thread from the ceiling of the porch.

"Probably he never ever has to take a bath."

"Don't be silly. Tatie must make him take baths. Tatie's very clean."

"Well, dirt doesn't show on him the way it does on me."

"*I* wouldn't want to be Charles. Probably he lives in a very little house. Probably he is very poor."

"That doesn't matter. He has more *fun* than I do. He says that when he's at home he can do almost anything he wants."

"Like what?"

"There's a dump near where he lives. Sometimes he goes to the dump and finds stuff. Once he found an old broken typewriter."

88

Jess made a face. "Who'd want an old broken type-writer?"

"Me."

"I wouldn't go to a dump anyway. I'd be scared."

"But not if you were a boy, Jess! Boys aren't scared. Charles isn't scared of anything. Charles wants to go up to the woods at the end of Autumn Street some-time, and I'm even scared to do that."

"You're not allowed to go that far anyway."

I sighed. "Even if I *could*, I'd be scared."

"Me too. But maybe when Daddy comes home from the war, he'll take us to the woods."

"We'll be *old* by then."

Jess sighed, too, when I said that. The war seemed to be going on forever. Summer seemed to be going on forever. Maybe I would be six years old forever.

"Liz," asked Jess suddenly, "have you ever heard of someone named Ferdie Gossett?"

Ferdie Gossett. I *had* heard of him. Charles had said "Let's scare Ferdie Gossett" when we still had the knife.

"Yes," I told her. "Charles said he's a crazy man who walks around town and talks to himself. Did you *see* him, Jess?"

Jessica nodded. "I went to the grocery store with Anne, and . . ."

"Oh, I *wish* I could cross streets, Jess!"

"When you start first grade you'll have to cross streets. That won't be very long. Anyway, Anne and I went down to the grocery store to get some eggs for her mother, because her mother wanted to make a cake. It was Anne's brother's birthday . . ."

"Jess. Tell about Ferdie Gossett!"

"I *am*. Right there at the grocery store—not inside the store, but outside, Liz, looking through the *trash* out in back—was this man with hair that I bet he has never combed in his whole entire life, and clothes so dirty that you can't imagine . . ."

"Was he talking to himself?"

Jess thought. "Yes, I think he was. But there was a cat, there, by the trash cans. Maybe he was talking to the cat."

"What was he saying?"

"I couldn't understand what he was saying. But he looked right at Anne and me when we came out of the store. He looked right at us. We ran. We almost dropped the eggs."

"Did he look at you as if he was friendly, or mean?"

"Neither one. As if he didn't even see us. As if he looked through us. It was really scary."

"How did you know his name?"

"Anne told me. She said he comes around the school a lot and stands by the playground, watching the kids. Everybody knows his name."

She started her embroidery again. I thought for a long time, about Ferdie Gossett.

"You know what, Jess? Probably he had a little child who died."

"Died?"

"Yes, because children die sometimes. Like Noah. And probably Ferdie Gossett's child died, and he feels so sad that he never combs his hair, and he likes to go and look at children playing."

"Well, maybe." Jess seemed dubious.

"I wouldn't be scared of him if I saw him. I think I would probably smile at him so he would feel better." I practiced a small, sad, piteous smile.

"I wouldn't." Jess shuddered.

"But it would be nice to have Charles with me, when I see Ferdie Gossett," I said. "Because Charles wouldn't be scared of him at *all*."

"Good morning, Elizabeth," Great-aunt Caroline said. "You've brought a friend, I see." She said it without raising her eyebrows, so I took Charles by the hand and led him into the aunts' cool green kitchen where translucent curtains suffused the sunlight and there were always grapes as pale as ghosts' eyes in a bowl.

"Charles, this is my Great-aunt Caroline. Great-aunt Caroline, this is Charles.

Charles stood gravely in the center of the kitchen, his brown legs below his shorts dusty with dirt that turned them beige, the opposite of the way that dirt affected my own scabbed knees.

"How do you do," he said, and held out his hand to Great-aunt Caroline, who took it firmly for a moment in her own.

"I'll call my sisters," Great-aunt Caroline said, "and we can all have some iced tea in the parlor. Isn't it hot? August always seems to be the hottest month, I think.

"Florence? Philippa? We have company!" she called up the stairs into the dim hallway above. I could hear their feet, soft as moths against a windowpane, as they came from their rooms.

"Today is Charles' birthday," I explained, when we were all seated in the parlor, Charles and I together on the crushed-velvet settee, our legs dangling. "And he came to visit Tatie because she made him a special cake with seven candles.

"Tatie is Charles' grandmother," I added, on the chance that the great-aunts might not know that.

Charles was not saying very much. But he was sipping his tall glass of iced tea politely.

"Well, my goodness, a birthday boy!" said Great-aunt Philippa. I had trouble, sometimes, telling the aunts apart. But Philippa was the one who wore a large diamond ring. She had been engaged, long ago, Tatie had told me, but the man had married someone else. The other aunts had never been engaged at all. I wondered if they were ever jealous of Philippa and her diamond ring that still, after so many years, sparkled the way wet spiderwebs did in sunshine. "And you're Tatie's grandson. Tell me, Charles, do you call her Grandmother, or do you call her Tatie the way we all do?"

"I calls her Tatie. She like that better."

"Sweet Potatie," I announced. "That's what Charles and I call her sometimes, just teasing."

"Her real name Titania," Charles said suddenly, to the great-aunts. I looked at him in astonishment. I had never known that before.

Great-aunt Florence sat up straight in her rocker with interest. "Titania! Why, that's Shakespeare! Did you know that, Charles?"

"No ma'am."

"Well, my goodness, that's from *A Midsummer Night's Dream!* Titania was Queen of the Fairies."

Charles sipped his tea. "I likes stories about fairies."

Great-aunt Florence leaned forward and looked at him more carefully. "Do you go to school, Charles?"

"No ma'am. I just be seven today. When Fall come, then I go to first grade."

"So you don't read yet, Charles?"

"No ma'am."

"*I* can read," I said.

"Philippa. Caroline. I've had a wonderful idea. Why couldn't we divide the parts, the three of us, and we could read *A Midsummer Night's Dream* to Charles. He says he likes stories about fairies. Now we can't do it today, Charles, because my sisters and I will need some time for preparation . . ."

"I taught myself to read when I was four," I said loudly, but no one seemed to be listening.

"I can come back," said Charles. He set his empty glass on the silver tray, took a pink linen napkin, and wiped his mouth carefully. I had already wiped my own mouth with the back of my hand.

"Yes, he can come back. We shall do that some day very soon, Charles." Great-aunt Florence leaned back, her eyes excited and planning.

"Don't we have some cupcakes left from Wednesday, Caroline?" asked Philippa. "It is Charles' birthday, after all."

They brought cupcakes, frosted with chocolate, baked in little pleated paper cups, on a flowered plate.

"Tatie, she make good cupcakes," said Charles, taking one. "But these cupcakes, they look as good as Tatie's."

Liar, I thought.

"My birthday is in March," I said. "So I will be the youngest person in the first grade, probably."

"When I go to school I going to learn to read right

away," said Charles to my great-aunts. "Then I going to get me a library card so I can read me lots of books."

The three great-aunts smiled, sighed, and rocked, looking at each other meaningfully, looking at Charles.

"There is a whole world of books waiting for you, Charles," said Great-aunt Caroline in her lilac voice. "What an exciting time you will have when you learn to read."

"Yes ma'am. I going to read me adventure stories."

They beamed.

"Florence. Philippa. Why don't we show Charles the *inclinator?* Why don't we give Charles a ride?"

I stood up, and cupcake crumbs fell from my lap to the rug. "That's not *fair.* You don't let Jess and me ride on the inclinator."

"Don't be rude, Elizabeth. Charles is a guest, and it is his birthday."

They left me standing there, and took Charles by the hand, to the stairway, where the mechanical seat, operated by a small switch, moved slowly up and down the stairs in its track against the wall. I stood in the doorway to the parlor, against the thick velvet curtains, and watched, pouting, while they helped Charles onto the seat and showed him how to turn the switch. They giggled when his eyes widened as it moved.

"Hold on tight, now, Charles!" called Great-aunt Florence as he began to move slowly up the stairs.

He rose to the top of the long staircase, sitting straight, grinning, his sneakered feet neatly together, until I could see only his legs, then only his feet, then nothing at all from my place in the doorway. I could hear the soft whir of the inclinator and, along with it, my great-aunts' delighted soft laughter.

"I be way at the top of the world!" called Charles from the dim beige place at the top of the stairs.

" 'Way at the top of the world' " repeated one of the great-aunts to the two others. They fluttered together like sparrows, looking upward, their papery faces pink with excitement.

"Here he comes, now!" called Great-aunt Caroline. And Charles whirred back down, his shoulders straight, his smile proud, his hand lightly on the switch, making the inclinator move.

When he dismounted, he bowed theatrically to my great-aunts, and they giggled in breathy spasms.

"We have to go now," I said, glumly.

We said our good-byes at the back door: or they did. I was silent. Charles shook hands gravely with each of the three sisters, who bobbed and tittered.

"Thank you very much," said Charles. "Your iced tea be very good, but sometimes it make it better if you put some mint leaf in it."

"My goodness," exclaimed Great-aunt Caroline. "I *did* forget the mint! Aren't you a nice boy, Charles, to remind me of that. When you come back, we shall surely have mint in our tea!"

We walked back to Grandfather's house silently through the dusty alley, kicking stones.

At the gate to Grandfather's yard, I turned to Charles and looked him straight in the eye.

"Happy birthday," I said, "nigger."

Charles grinned.

Though August, as Great-aunt Caroline had said, seemed to be the hottest month of the summer, the nights began to be cool. The summer slipcovers were still on the parlor furniture the rainy August night that Grandfather said, after the evening news, "I believe it's a good night for a fire."

I shivered. I remembered Grandfather's fires from winter, and there was a magic to them. There was the placement of the birch logs. The careful rolling of newspaper. The lighting, with a special long match.

I was not allowed to do any of that, only to watch Grandfather. Later, when the fire was dying, I would be permitted to throw in one of the pine cones that were kept in a special basket. But that would be after Grandfather's magic.

"May I hold Gordon?" I asked Mama. "I want to show him the fire." She placed the baby in my arms as I sat on the rug in front of the fireplace.

Gordon had become less boring. He cried less now, smelled of spitup less often, and held his head high, looking around with blue, unfocused eyes. Sometimes he smiled at me. The grownups said that he looked like Daddy, and I wondered how they knew that, how they could remember, when I couldn't, my father's face.

Of Gordon's few baby skills there was only one that I admired. Sometimes, when Mama bathed him, I watched as he lay squirming and naked in her arms, and sometimes he peed into the air, high and arched like a rainbow, the thin stream bright against the sunny window behind him.

"I wish I could do that," I confided in Mama. She smiled.

"Well, you're a girl. Girls can't do that." I already knew that they couldn't. I had tried, myself, privately, in the bathtub, and met with humiliating failure.

"Can Daddy do that?"

"Goodness. I suppose he could."

"Charles can."

"Elizabeth! You haven't . . ."

I caught my error quickly. "Oh, no. I haven't *seen* him do it. But I meant that I suppose all boys can."

But I was lying. I *had* seen Charles do it, often, behind the lilacs. He aimed at ants.

I held Gordon, drowsy and powdered, on my lap, and played with his hands in the firelight. The flames licked the dry logs and snapped; sparks drifted up the chimney; a log shifted and fell.

"Do the magic, Grandfather. Do the magic for Gordon."

So Grandfather leaned forward, took a handful of his magic sand from its box, and sprinkled it onto the fire. For a few moments the flames turned blue, green, purple—for a few moments I saw in the fire all the colors of my paintings, my skies and mountains and hills, moving, alive, flickering and dancing against each other. Blending, the way I had blended my land-scapes. There was sky in the fireplace. There was the Pacific, the horizon, the war, the past: the pale blue of places I had dreamed of; and the dark, awesome greens of places to which I was frightened to go.

The magic was over so quickly. It always was. The baby shifted in my lap and whimpered.

"Grandfather, do you want to hold Gordon?"

But Grandfather was standing, as startled as if the magic were new to him, as puzzled as if he had seen none of us before, as if the firelight were frightening and strange. His face was a face I had never seen.

"I am not well," he said slowly. He turned and left the room.

From the hallway, as the clock on the stairs struck, we heard the sound as he fell.

Stroke.

Stroke.

When I was told, the next day, after the hushed voices, the confusion, the fear were over, that Grandfather had had a stroke, I associated it with the clock. He had had a stroke of eight.

I avoided the clock as much as I could. Its strokes, which had always signaled news time, bedtime, now were connected with the evil, the fear I felt when I heard Grandfather fall. The clock measured out dying, I knew, although Grandfather was not dead; the clock waited, and one day it would strike—STROKE—again.

The painted face of the moon at the top of the tall clock continued to smile.

The fire had faded untended, and I had not thrown my pine cone in. And the magic, Grandfather's magic, was sealed in the small box still. I opened it secretly, alone in the parlor while Grandfather was in the hospital, and looked inside; there was only gray sand, no colors, none of the bright blues and greens. It took a magic Grandfather to make the fire colors happen; and Grandfather had crumpled on the hall rug. His powers were gone.

I watched new powers come to Grandmother, who had never had a child. Now, when Grandfather came home and the big house was newly equipped with hospital bed, with wheelchair, and all the chrome trappings of illness, Grandmother became a mother for the first time.

"Try this, dear," she said, in a soft, mother's voice that I had never heard her use before, as she held a spoonful of applesauce to his lopsided mouth. She wiped his chin with a cloth napkin. She looked at him with the fond look that Mama gave to Gordon, and Grandfather's eyes were as unfocused and trusting as the baby's, looking back at her.

There was a covered enamel pail, tall and white, in Grandfather's bedroom, and I could not bring myself, even when he was on the porch in his wheelchair and the room was empty, to look inside the pail. I knew there were diapers there.

So it was not death to be feared as much as this other. The going backward. No one spoke of it. And I thought again of my cousin David, whom I remembered still as tanned and playful in summer, laughing as he chased me to torture me with tickles. After two years of war, David was still in the hospital. No one had spoken of him, either, for a long time.

Finally I asked, "Did David have a stroke, too?"

Mama looked at me, puzzled. "David? Do you remember David?"

As if I could have forgotten that green, sweet summer when I was three. "He used to tickle me and call me Dizzy Lizzie," I reminded her. "Did he have a stroke, like Grandfather?" I didn't remember David's face, any more than I remembered Daddy's; but I could remember the hugs and the sunlight that summer. If, in his hospital, David was diapered now, and someone was wiping spit from his chin, I wanted to know.

But Mama said no. "David was shell-shocked," she said.

I didn't let her see that the words terrified me more than the word *stroke*. In Great-aunt Caroline's bedroom there was a pink translucent shell on a dresser; once she had held it to my ear and told me that I could hear the ocean.

"Can I hear the Pacific?" I had asked, turning my head against the curved surface to find the sound.

"Yes," Great-aunt Caroline had said. "The sound of the waves."

I wasn't sure, because I had never heard waves. I

heard a hollow pink sound like the sound of far away, like the sound of dreams.

Now David was there, shocked, in the hollow void, and it was worse than Grandfather, whose cane stood unused in the hallway closet, and whose mouth formed no words but opened wetly again and again. David's fate had to do with the war; and the shell made it the war in the Pacific, so I had new fears for Daddy. Everyone I loved was threatened by things I didn't understand. Everyone but Tatie. I wandered down the stairs and into the kitchen; Tatie was there, as she always was, and she was making a pie. Apple pie was so familiar, so comforting, that I forgot the sickroom upstairs, forgot David, the shell, the Pacific, and Daddy, settled myself on a kitchen chair and popped a fingerful of raw dough into my mouth.

"Grandmother says that if you eat raw dough your insides will stick together. Do you believe that, Tatie?"

"Nope. I been eating it myself since I was as big as you."

"How are your insides?"

"Too *fat* is how they are. And yours is too skinny."

"Grandmother says that if I want to grow properly I should take cod-liver oil and learn the Prayer for the Whole State of Christ's Church."

"Ha."

"That's what I say. Ha."

"Lick your finger, Liz, and hold it out."

I did, dutifully, and Tatie sprinkled my fingertip with cinnamon. I sucked it while she sprinkled the sliced apples; it tasted like Fall, and made my nose itch.

"Tatie, if I ask you something will you promise to say yes?"

"Nope."

"Please?"

"Ask me."

"Can I take the can of cinnamon, just for a few minutes?"

"Where you want to take it to?"

I kicked my dangling feet together, and finally told her. "Grandfather's in his wheelchair on the upstairs porch. I want to put cinnamon on his finger."

"Your grandma's with him, and she won't like that."

"If I ask her first, and she says yes, can I?"

Tatie sighed and handed me the small tin can.

But Grandmother was asleep, nodding in her wicker chair, a book open on her lap and her glasses pushed up on top of her gray hair. I tiptoed to where Grandfather sat staring in his wheelchair, a blanket across his legs despite the end-of-summer heat, his eyes alive but uncomprehending, his hands useless in his covered lap.

"Lick your finger and hold it out," I whispered to him.

His head bobbed but his hands didn't move. His mouth fell open and made shapes but no sounds came. He looked at me. I remembered him walking, in his crisp white suit, carrying his cane, on Autumn Street, and was sad.

"I'll do it for you," I whispered, and took his hand gently. I put his forefinger into my own mouth, and tasted his clean, aged skin. Carefully I sprinkled cinnamon on his damp fingertip and lifted it to the wet black shape that had once been his fine proud mouth. It touched his tongue, and with his mouth he shaped what I understood to be a smile. I dried his finger with the hem of my dress, put his hand back into his lap, and crept away. Grandmother never knew.

Lillian Chestnut had boyfriends who were soldiers. Sometimes Jess and I watched when she came down from her over-the-garage bedroom in the early evenings, dressed in full gathered skirts and off-the-shoulder blouses, and went out the back door to be met at the corner by soldiers who arrived in a rattletrap car.

When I called Daddy a soldier once, Mama corrected me.

"Your father's an officer," she said.

"But he's in the army. People in the army are soldiers. And people in the navy are sailors." I had learned that much, I thought, from *Life* magazine.

"Some of them are. But there are also officers, and your father is an officer."

"What's the difference?"

Mama sighed. "Oh, Liz, it's very complicated."

That meant that she wasn't going to explain it to me.

Even with my memory of Daddy vague and distant, I could tell that Lillian's boyfriends were different. They came from the army base just outside of town, and were young and noisy, with cigarettes attached to the corners of their mouths. Lillian always looked nervously over her shoulder toward the house as she went out to their car; we could hear her say, "Will you guys *hush?*" with suppressed laughter in her voice before they drove away.

By early evening Grandmother was always upstairs, on the other side of the house, spooning soup into Grandfather, or reading Dickens aloud. Mama would be in her own room, preparing the baby for bed and listening to the evening news on a small radio. The evenings of Chinese Checkers and firelight were over.

"That Lillian," Tatie said to Jess and me after we had watched one evening's leave-taking from the back porch, "she gonna get in trouble, goin' with soldiers."

Getting into trouble was old hat with me. "Maybe,"

I acknowledged enviously. "But she's old enough. She can't get punished."

"Ha. Her kind of trouble carry its own punishment."

From the time I had deliberately rubbed poison ivy on myself, I knew that there were kinds of behavior that carried their own punishments, but it was hard to relate that experience to Lillian driving off every evening with loud-voiced soldiers.

"Well," I said, affecting worldliness, "at least she won't get all swollen up and feeling horrible."

"Ha," said Tatie, putting the last of the dinner dishes away.

*

One evening Charles was there. He and I sat on the back steps before bedtime, counting the fireflies in the yard, slapping at the mosquitoes, planning what we would do in the morning. Lillian appeared with her hair freshly curled and her waist cinched in by a wide red belt. She lit a cigarette and sat with us on the steps, watching the road for the car full of soldiers.

"Lillian," I asked her, "what happened to that one soldier who used to come, the one with red hair who called you 'Roasted Chestnut'?"

Lillian laughed and took a long drag on her cigarette. The smoke appeared in two streams from her nose, like a horse breathing in winter.

"Red? He's gone. He's fighting the damn Germans."

"I thought the war was against the Japanese. My father's fighting the Japanese."

Charles groaned. "Elizabeth Jane, you so *stupid.*"

Lillian aimed a smoke ring at me so that I could poke my finger through it. Then she did one for Charles.

"It's against the Japanese *and* the Germans. Some of the guys go one place, some go another."

"Which is worse?"

Lillian lifted her shoulders slightly. "I don't know. The Japs chop heads off. But the Germans put people in ovens."

Her words came out into the still evening and the fireflies continued to blink; but my own eyes were wide open and my stomach was seized with cramps.

"Is that really true, Lillian?"

"Yeah. You can see it in the newsreels. Oh, I forgot. You're not allowed to go to movies, are you?"

"No." No wonder. I had been taken to *Snow White.* I had thought all movies were like *Snow White.*

"Charles, did you know that, about the ovens and the chopping heads off?" I asked.

"Yeah," Charles lied. His eyes were as wide in the early darkness as mine.

"Lillian, Hugo Hoffman was a German," I told her, making my voice as meaningful as Grandmother's.

"Who's Hugo Hoffman?" She lit another cigarette, putting the stub of the first into her purse so that Grandmother wouldn't find it in the yard.

"Next door. Remember when the little boy next door died? His father was German."

"Yeah?"

"At the beginning of the war he disappeared."

"No kidding. Where'd he disappear to?"

"Nobody knows. When the war started he just went off in the night and nobody ever saw him again."

Lillian was interested. "And then the kid died. What'd he die of?"

My stomach cramped again. "Pneumonia, the doctor said."

"The doctor *said*. I wonder about *that,* let me tell you. There's all sorts of strange stuff goes on. I bet anything that guy is a spy for the Germans."

Suddenly we were talking in whispers, in secret voices. Even Charles.

"Spies is over there, where the war is. They ain't in a little ole town like *this,*" he whispered.

Lillian blew smoke out again and looked impatiently down the street for her ride. Then she said in a hushed, ominous voice, "Don't you kid yourself. Spies are all over, and the walls have ears. There are

German radio operators right in this town, let me tell you. Out in California there are thousands of Japs with radios, signaling subs. There isn't a safe place left. And the only thing you can do about it"—she rose, as the sound of the noisy car came—"is go out and have fun. Right?"

"Right," said Charles.

"Right," I echoed. We both waved toward the car as she left, but it was dark now; the only things we could see were the small glowing circles of cigarettes, redder than fireflies. From the kitchen Tatie called to us to come in.

*

"Charles," I whispered to him in the morning, as we stood in the backyard, "do you believe what Lillian said about spies?"

"Yeah."

"What're spies?"

He hesitated. "People who fight for the other side."

"How can they fight for the Germans, here in this town? What did she mean about radios? *Everybody* has radios. *We* have a radio."

"It's a special kind of spy radio they have. They talk to Hitler."

I knew about Hitler, vaguely. Hitler was an enemy. "Do you think Hugo Hoffman talks to Hitler?"

Charles sat on the grass and thought. "You know

what, Elizabeth? That Hoffman house, she's got a big attic. Look at all them windows."

I looked up. All of the houses on Autumn Street were very large. They all had attics.

"So what?"

"I bet that Hugo Hoffman, he been up in that attic all the time, talking to Hitler."

I knew that it couldn't be true. If Hugo Hoffman had been in the attic the day that Noah cried and called out, the day that Nathaniel and I had held the duck race, Hugo Hoffman would have come down, spy or no spy. But I didn't want to tell Charles about that.

"He couldn't be. He'd starve."

"Elizabeth Jane, you so . . ."

"I am *not* stupid, Charles. Nobody can live in an attic and not eat. And how would he go to the bathroom? There aren't any bathrooms in attics."

Charles explained it to me patiently, the way my Sunday School teacher went through things again and again, making me feel unbearably ignorant.

"He creeps down at night, after everybody asleep, and eats and pees. His wife, she probably knows he's there. Spies, they can tell their wife, but nobody else."

I looked again, nervously, at the Hoffmans' attic windows, wondering if Nathaniel's father could possibly be there, chatting with Hitler. The Autumn

Street attics were very hot in summer, and there was a wasp's nest in Grandfather's.

"Charles," I said slowly, terrified by my own daring, "Mrs. Hoffman took Nathaniel to Harrisburg this morning, to buy clothes for school. And she always leaves the back door unlocked."

Charles grinned. He was always looking for something exciting to do, and I still refused to go with him to the woods. "You wanna go in?"

"What if he heard us?"

"We gotta make a plan. We go in in our bare feet so we don't make no noise. Then we creeps up the stairs without no noise, and we creeps all the way up to the attic door and we listen."

"What do we do if we hear him?"

Charles thought. "We call the army and tell them."

"Charles, what if he knows that Mrs. Hoffman and Nathaniel are gone, and he comes down in the house and sees us?"

"Elizabeth Jane, you don't know yet that spies is serious stuff. He staying in that attic all the time because if he comes out except when it be real dark, somebody might see him through the windows. No, he gonna stay right in that attic in daytime, tapping at his radio to Hitler."

"What will the army do to him?"

"Kill him. They always kills spies. First they torture them some."

"I don't want anybody to be killed."

"Long as he sits there talking to Hitler, people getting put into them ovens. You like that better?"

I remembered Red, with his quick, cocky voice, calling softly to Lillian as she got into the car, "Hey there, Roasted Chestnut!" I didn't want Red to be in an oven, trussed like a turkey, with juices oozing pink from the prick-marks in the browning skin. It was the vision of Red in a baking pan, a cigarette still propped in his grin, that made me agree to go into Hoffman's house.

We slipped through the opening in the hedge, glancing back to be sure that Tatie wasn't watching, that Grandmother had not appeared on the porch to check the roses, or that Mama was not bringing the baby to the yard for some sun. But the house was silent, closed, and uncaring.

The Hoffmans' back door was, as I knew it would be, unlocked. The kitchen was sunny and neat, the breakfast dishes washed and draining in the sink, a bowl of bananas on the table next to a bottle of vitamins. Nathaniel's treasured stack of Captain Marvel comics was on a shelf beside the telephone; I saw Charles eye them greedily, and I nudged him forward through the kitchen. The floor was cool and clean, recently scrubbed, against our bare feet. The only sounds were the loud ticking of an ornate clock in the dining room and the stealthy brush of our feet on the rug as we passed through on our way to the stairs.

But even empty rooms are populated with the presence of those recently there. I thought that I could smell the thin flowery scent of the cologne Mrs. Hoffman sometimes wore; and I could almost hear the soft laughter of Nathaniel as he played. I grabbed for Charles' hand and held it tight; he turned to me and formed some words with his mouth.

"What?" I whispered.

"Shhh." He formed the words again, adding a little breath to them so that I could understand. "Look for *clues.*"

Clues? I didn't know what he meant. Surely there would be no evidence of Hugo Hoffman's presence here in the empty first floor. Then I stiffened and pulled Charles back into the dining room. I pointed to the large carved wooden clock on the buffet.

Charles looked at me, puzzled, and I remembered that he couldn't read.

"Made in Germany," I whispered, pointing to the words.

He raised his eyebrows, praising me with the look. It was a clue.

At the foot of the stairs, Charles whispered to me. "We should've brung the knife."

I shook my head. I wanted no part of the knife. I had even, when Charles wasn't there, rearranged the leaves and stones over its burial place so that we couldn't find the spot again.

Still clutching his hand, I tiptoed beside Charles up the staircase to the second floor. I had never been upstairs in the house before, but the rooms seemed familiar. There was a guest room; I knew the tidy, unused look of a guest room from Grandfather's house, which had five such impersonal spaces, their closets empty but for a few wire hangers.

Nathaniel's room was messy, bright-colored, haphazard and happy, strewn with little-boy toys. Lincoln logs and a half-constructed, green-roofed cabin lay on the rug, waiting for his return, for his cheerful concentration. I felt the guilt of gladness once again, that Noah was dead, that Nathaniel's playthings were safe, and that Nathaniel smiled so much now. I dropped Charles' hand, knelt on the rug, and added a green slat to the roof of the little house.

Nathaniel's pajamas, printed with clowns and jugglers, were discarded in a corner of the room, dropped in a wrinkled heap where they were outlined by a rectangle of sunlight from the window.

The door to what had been Noah's room was closed. I could hear again his high-pitched wail as it had come through the opened window of that room in June, and once again my half-meant prayer of apology to a god disguised as my father, and to the Hoffmans, crept through my consciousness like a bewildered kitten. When Charles made a motion with his hand toward the doorknob of that room, I stopped him decisively, shaking my head no.

Mrs. Hoffman's bedroom, at the front of the house, was prettily decorated with blue flowered fabrics; a quilted satin comforter was folded into a scrupulous triangle at the foot of the double bed. On the bureau, in a gold filigreed frame, a tinted photograph of the twins, dressed in Eton suits, smiled eerily at me. I nudged Charles and pointed to the other photograph, to the grave face of a wavy-haired man who I knew must be Hugo Hoffman. Charles studied it and nodded, apparently designating it a further clue.

As I glanced at some papers on Mrs. Hoffman's bedside table, Charles ventured across the room. Turning, I almost giggled aloud. He was balancing in a pair of high-heeled shoes with ankle straps and gaudy red bows; his bare, brown ankles converged as he tried tentatively to walk across the rug. He grinned, acknowledging his own foolishness in gleeful silence, and returned the shoes carefully to the floor of the open closet. We went into the hall to find the attic stairs.

It surprised us both that the stairs were open; there was no furtively closed door to which we could press our ears against a keyhole and listen for the spy speaking in low-voiced German. There were no sounds at all from the attic, and the stairs were piled with dusty cardboard boxes, one marked "Christmas tree ornaments" and another "Patterns—size 6—Twins." A mop stood upended in a bucket; and farther up, I saw, with a twinge of pain, a folded, mildewed yellow slicker and a small pair of red rubber boots that I recognized as Noah's.

I was no longer frightened or excited. I was simply sad and ashamed, anxious to get away from the Hoffmans' house and from their lives. I was angry at Charles for having suggested the adventure and angry with myself that the suggestion could have enticed me into a place whose woeful secrets were so small, so despairing, and so private.

"Come on," I said aloud. "Let's go."

Charles was still caught up in the intrigue. "Shhh," he whispered, alarmed by my voice.

"Come *on*." I pulled away from him, hurried down the stairs and toward the back door. He followed me, and our two sets of bare feet thumped through the empty house, made slapping sounds on the kitchen linoleum, and finally felt the safety of the yard, the hedge opening, and the familiar soft-shorn grass of our own territory.

"You was dumb to make all that noise," Charles scolded me. "He could still be in the basement. We didn't listen at the basement door."

"He isn't there at all."

"You don't know. Spies has all sorts of ways to keep themselves secret."

"He isn't there. On the table by Mrs. Hoffman's bed there was a letter."

"What'd it say?"

"It was in an envelope. I didn't take it out. But on the envelope it said that it was from Hugo Hoffman, Denver, Colorado."

"Where's that?"

"I don't know, but it isn't Pennsylvania."

"Well, he's probably bein' a spy there, wherever it is. Lillian said there was spies everywhere."

"Old dumb Lillian. I wish they'd put *her* in an oven."

"Yeah, then she *really* be a Roasted Chestnut!"

I pulled up a handful of Grandfather's grass and threw it impulsively at Charles. "Good-for-nothing old Charles!" I said, and giggled.

He spat the green shreds from his mouth, tore a

handful from the lawn to throw back at me, and cried, "No-account ole Elizabeth!"

We lay side by side on Grandfather's lawn, helpless with laughter and freckled with fragments of grass. When you love someone, I thought, you can be *bad* together sometimes. How I loved Charles then.

"Well, why *can't* Charles go to my school?"

"Hold still, Liz. I can't braid your hair when you're wiggling that way." Mama criss-crossed the strands of blond hair deftly and decorated the ends with new blue hair ribbons to match my dress. "Charles lives in a different part of town, that's why. He'll go to a school near his house, and you're going to the Jefferson School near *this* house."

"But I won't know anybody if Charles isn't there. I don't want to go."

"Don't be silly, Elizabeth. You know Jessica. You know Anne, and Nathaniel Hoffman. All the children from Autumn Street will be at Jefferson School."

"They're all older than me. Charles is the only first-grade person I know."

"Well, you'll meet other children at school. You'll make new friends."

"Why can't Charles live here, in Tatie's room, and then he can go to my school?"

"*Elizabeth.* Hold *still.* There; your dress is buttoned. Can you tie your shoes yourself?"

"Yes," I pouted, "but I don't want to. I don't want to go to school. Not unless Charles does."

Mama turned the hairbrush to its flat silver side and swatted my behind. "Stop it, Elizabeth. You are going to school, and that's that. Jess is waiting for you downstairs. Don't forget to get your lunch from Tatie. You're going to be late if you don't go *right now.*"

I tied my shoes and stomped off, glowering. Then I turned in the doorway, went back, and hugged Mama.

"I'm sorry."

"It's all right, sweetheart. You're just scared. Now go on, and have a good day."

I plodded down the stairs and muttered, out of Mama's hearing, "I am *not* scared."

It was a lie, of course, but if I said it to myself often enough, I could make myself believe it.

*

The Jefferson School was brick, tall, and Gothic, rising incongruously from an entire block of flat asphalt. Jessica walked with me and tried dutifully to explain the rules of going to school, but she interrupted herself again and again to wave to friends. Jess had finished third grade at Jefferson the previous year. She had friends. She knew all the rules. And Jess never questioned rules, as I did, even now, trudging dispiritedly beside her on the first day of school.

"That's the playground," Jessica said, waving her arm to indicate the expanse of gray asphalt as we approached. Then her wave shifted when she saw a dark-haired girl across the street. "Hi, Ruth Ann!"

"How can you *play* when there's no grass or trees?" I muttered.

"There's recess in the morning and again in the afternoon. That side over there is the girls' side, and this side is the boys' side. Now don't ever go onto the boys' side, Liz, or you'll get into trouble."

"You mean you can't play with boys at recess?"

"Of course not. You have to stay on the girls' side. You can draw hopscotches on the playground, but you have to bring your own chalk from home. You're not allowed to take the school chalk outside. Hi, Betsy!" She waved again to a girl in a plaid dress.

I sighed. I was no good at all at hopscotch, which Jess and her friends had played all summer on Autumn Street. I couldn't balance well on one leg; I stepped on the lines. They only let me play if there was no one else.

"Walk with us, Jess!"

"I can't. I have to take my sister in. Tomorrow I'll walk with you." She was calling across the street, to strangers.

"Jess, do you mean you won't walk with me tomorrow?"

"Elizabeth, you're a first grader. I can't walk to school with a first grader every day. You'll find somebody your own age to walk with. Now, look. This is the door we go in. I go upstairs, to fourth grade, but the first grade room is right here. Over there are the bathrooms—that's the boys', and this is the girls'. But if you have to go to the bathroom, you have to ask the teacher first."

I clung to her arm and could tell that she was anxious to leave me. "Jess," I whispered, "do you mean I have to tell the teacher if I have to go to the *bathroom?*"

"Yes. Let go of me."

"I can't tell the teacher that."

126

"Be a camel, then. Now let go. I can't be late."

She pried me loose and pushed me into the first grade room.

A tall young woman in a flowered dress knelt beside me so that her face was level with mine, and she was smiling. "Good morning," she said in a voice as warm and soft as bedroom slippers. "Did you come all alone on the very first day?"

I dispensed with Jessica in a nod. "Yes," I said.

"My goodness, you're *very brave*. Most children need to have their mothers bring them, and even then" —she lowered her voice to a whisper—"some of them cry. I'm so glad to have a big girl like you in my class. What's your name?"

"Elizabeth Jane Lorimer."

"Mine's Miss MacDonald. Look, Elizabeth. Right here on this desk is your name. I've made special nametags for all my first graders. Would you like to sit here in your desk and look at some books while I greet the other children?"

I nodded. First grade didn't seem so bad after all. The shelves around the room were filled with books, books with pictures on the covers, more intriguing than the leather-bound volumes at Grandfather's house. Miss MacDonald brought me some.

At the desk next to mine, a dark-haired girl sat leafing through a large book of bright illustrations. I read the nametag on her desk: LOUISE. She glanced over and grinned impishly at me.

"These are baby books," she whispered. "Look—there aren't even any *words.*"

"Can you read?" I asked.

"Yeah. I can already read pretty good."

"Me too. But probably the other kids can't. That's why they have to have baby books."

"Yeah. Because of the other kids." She grinned again.

The other kids. I liked the phrase when it came from Louise. I had a friend already.

After school, we traded sweaters and walked together. She wore the blue sweater that Great-aunt Florence had knitted for me, and I wore her yellow one buttoned up over my blue and white striped dress. We exchanged telephone numbers, agreed to bring our jump ropes to school the next day and to approach Miss MacDonald together and ask for books with words. On the sidewalk ahead of us, I saw Jessica, walking and laughing with two other girls, their arms intertwined.

"That's my sister," I told Louise. "The pretty one with the curly hair.

"Hi, Jess!" I called.

Jessica looked back, smiled, and waved to me. Then

she turned back to her friends; I took Louise's hand in mine and we kicked the few leaves that had begun to fall, with our first-day-of-school shoes, giggling. The air smelled like apple cider, sweet and fresh.

*

I saw Ferdie Gossett for the first time, at school, and forgot my intention to smile shyly at him. It terrified me that he was there, almost every recess, standing by the edge of the playground. His eyes seemed hooded, like a reptile's, and his sloping chin disappeared into a neck that was wrapped in layers of clothes as stained and repulsive as old bandages. But the other children were unafraid of his presence. They said he had always been there. They pronounced his name Ferdiegossett, the way we all slurred phrases like peanutbutter and bestfriend. Sometimes they pelted him with pebbles, the tiny weapons as casually cruel as the small insults that we inflicted on each other at play.

It frightened me that his inaudibly moving mouth and his vacant eyes made me think of my grandfather.

He became part of my mind's landscape of school, as omnipresent as asphalt, as reliable as chalk. Like snapshots glued to pages of an album, my images of school were objects and people: Ticonderoga pencils in an orderly yellow row; a daub of mint-scented paste on a square of construction paper; Miss MacDonald in a flowered dress, bending to whisper; furry erasers thick with chalk dust; Dick and Jane and Baby Sally skipping through the pages of a book; Ferdie Gossett, reptilian sentinel of the playground; and Louise Donohue, bold and mischievous, who moved into the spot that Charles had occupied alone, and became my other best friend.

"Charles," I said to him tentatively one weekend when he came to visit Tatie, "I can't play with you *all* day, only part. Because I have to visit my friend Louise."

"I don't care," said Charles. But his eyes were hurt.

"You probably have new friends at your school," I said warily, not certain whether I wanted him to or not.

"Yeah. Clarence E. Cartwright. He's my friend at school."

"And if I came to visit you at your house, probably you would have to go play with Clarence E. Cartwright some of the time."

"You never come visit me at my house," Charles pointed out, as if the idea startled him.

"Well. If I did. If I was allowed to."

"Yeah. Probly I wouldn't even play with you at *all*, if you did."

"I wouldn't care," I lied.

"Me neither. Clarence E. Cartwright and me, we don't like girls any."

"Oh. I like *you* still, Charles."

We looked at each other anxiously. Finally he reached into his pocket. "I brung you something," he said. "Jest my ole printing paper."

I looked at his neat printing, the rows of uppercase *A*s and *B*s, and at the star pasted on the top of the perfect paper. His penciled letters were as carefully formed as my own. It seemed a link between our different schools, our different lives.

"Thank you," was all that I could think of to say.

*

Louise's house was very different from Grandfather's. Instead of the austere silence punctuated by the hollow striking of the hall clock, there was noise at the Donohues' house: radios played in adjacent rooms, tuned to different stations, combinations of gospel music, syncopated Rinso White! Rinso Bright! commercials, and the portentous conversations of Helen Trent and her many lovers.

Instead of the gleaming, well-polished antiques, each placed in the spot, at the angle, at which it would stand forever, there was clutter at Louise's house, and the surprise of things moved, rearranged, discarded, or changed.

One week there was a canary in a cage in the Donohues' kitchen; he hopped and twittered and sang and spewed seed on the stained linoleum floor. He had several names. Louise called him Goldie. Her mother had named him Rudy Vallee, after a singer, and she called him Rudy for short. Cousins who came and went referred to the canary as Yellowbird and Tweety; the same cousins called Louise things like Weezie, and Lulubelle, and Babydoll.

One afternoon the door to the canary's cage was left open by mistake, and the little bird emerged, looked around, flew across the kitchen, sang briefly by an open window, and disappeared. The Donohues waited a day or two, hoping he might return, decided cheerfully that he would not, filled the cage with artificial flowers, and hung it in another room.

The casual, amiable impermanence of everything delighted me.

There were babies at Louise's, but they were not like my own baby brother, who slept according to a schedule and was brought out for display only occasionally, always in clean clothes and with his sparse blond hair brushed into a temporary curl. Louise's baby brothers were one and two years old; they sat most of the time together in a playpen with their hands full of soggy graham crackers that they fed alternately to themselves and to each other. Their diapers were always wet, and each baby had a pink rash at the back of his neck. Louise's mother called it "heat rash" and sprinkled it from time to time with cornstarch from the kitchen cupboard. Their nostrils were always crusty, but they smiled a lot when they weren't biting each other, and they reached their sticky, smeared hands up to me when I came to the house. I liked the babies.

"Hi, Ralph. Hi, Frank," I always said to them shyly, avoiding their gluey grasps and refusing their offers of wet cookies.

Louise's room was a collection of her entire six years of life. She still had her own baby clothes, now on an assortment of eyeless, stuffing-leaky dolls that were piled in a corner.

"Was that yours, really? Did you wear that?" I asked her, fascinated, when she showed me an embroidered white dress, stiff now with dirt, on her favorite, largest doll.

"Yeah. In the album there's a picture of me wearing that. 'Louise Marie, at Aunt Monica's, age six months,' it says under the picture. My mom writes everything in white ink, in the album, because the pages are black."

My mother, too, wrote with white ink in our photograph albums, dipping the pen again and again. There were pictures of me, too, at six months, wearing white embroidered dresses. But where had those dresses gone? Our baby had new clothes, and my dolls were dressed in my mother's carefully stitched doll clothes. What had happened to the things I remembered from

133

New York? My special glass with the red dots painted on the sides, from which I had drunk orange juice in the mornings? At Grandfather's house, orange juice was served in stemmed crystal, and I had not thought of my red-dotted glass until I met Louise and was introduced to lives that paid no attention to style but still cherished tattered and derelict memories. Maybe my special glass had been broken. Certainly the fragile crystal ones were more elegant.

But I wished that I had the thick, spotted glass to hold, still, for recollection's sake.

People shouted at each other, at Louise's house. Anger, grief, joy: all were conveyed at full volume, with gusto that nudged any tentative secrets out of corners for scrutiny.

"What's your grandfather's name?" Louise's mother had asked me when we met and I explained where I lived.

"I don't know," I confessed.

"YOU DON'T KNOW?" As if she had turned her volume dial to its full capacity.

"Well, I've always just called him Grandfather," I explained.

"Louise calls her grandfather Paw-Paw. But she better know his *name* if anyone asks her. Hey, Louise, what's Paw-Paw's name?"

"Ralph Cedric O'Reilly."

"Right. Now, Elizabeth, you find out what your grandfather's real name is, because sometime you might need to know it. In case you get hit by a car and the police have to call your mother, how would they know where to call?"

Hit by a *car?* I always looked both ways, several times, before I crossed the quiet streets on my way to school. If I were in a place of busy streets, my mother was with me, and I was holding her hand. But that evening I asked my mother what Grandfather's name was. She smiled, surprised that I didn't know.

"Benjamin Lord Creighton," she said, and showed me how to spell it. Benjamin and Lord (how *embarrassing,* to be named Lord) I could have spelled myself, sounding out the letters, but Creighton was impossible.

I told Louise's mother. "I found out what my grandfather's name is."

"Oh? So tell."

"Benjamin Creighton." No need to include the other.

"Oh." She wiped vigorously at some dishes with a spotted, damp towel, leaned over and wiped the babies' mouths with the same towel, and picked up the dishes again. "Oh. Well. How about *that!*"

How about that. She seemed embarrassed by my grandfather's name. Embarrassment at Louise's house always took the form of loudness and remarks like "how about that." I remembered that Louise's grandfather had shuffled into the kitchen once, a cigar in his mouth and his fly open. I had averted my eyes and begun to talk to the babies; but Louise's mother had laughed and said, "Hey, Paw-Paw, your barn door's open!" Paw-Paw had bellowed in response, "Well. How about that, anyway! What do you know," ostentatiously, pretending he didn't care; but he had been embarrassed. He turned his back and fumbled with the buttons, puffing hastily on the cigar so that thick smoke rose around his head as if he were trying to create a diversion or a screen.

"So," said Louise's mother, after I had given her my grandfather's name. "Your mother was Celia Creighton, then. I remember her from when we were both little girls. I should have guessed who you were: you look like your mama did when she was little."

It couldn't be true, I thought. Mama's hair was curly, like Jessica's, and always in place. Mama had graceful hands and clothes that were clean. She could never have looked like me. Neither Grandfather nor Tatie had ever told me that she did.

"What was my mother like when she was little?" I asked Louise's mother.

"Pretty. She had beautiful clothes—I remember a yellow dress she had, with a deep blue sash around the waist. I used to think it was the most beautiful dress in the world."

I knew that feeling. There was a girl in the first grade who sometimes wore a pink dress with hearts embroidered on the pockets. I felt that if I owned that dress I would be beautiful; but the feeling made me dislike the girl. I realized that Louise's mother must have disliked mine, if only for the yellow, blue-sashed dress.

"And she had a pony, too. There was a little stable there where your grandfather's garage is, now."

So. That cinched it. Louise's mother must have *hated* mine. I would hate any little girl who had her own pony.

I tried to make up for that justifiable hatred. I told Louise's mother, "Her mother died when she was born, so she was practically an orphan. Probably that's why they got her a pony."

"Yeah. I knew that, that she didn't have a mother. A maid used to walk her to school when she was little. Then when she got older, she went away to boarding school someplace. She was the only one in town who went away to boarding school. So she didn't have many friends here. I used to feel sorry for her."

Feel *sorry* for the girl with the yellow dress and the pony? *I* wouldn't have. I looked at Louise's mother with a new respect. She was kinder than I would ever be.

"My mother doesn't have very many friends here now, either, because she stays at home with the baby all the time. Why don't you come to visit her someday?"

The invitation embarrassed Mrs. Donohue, and her volume control went up again. "WELL. THAT'S SOME INVITATION. YOU HEAR THAT, LOUISE? ELIZABETH WANTS ME TO VISIT HER MOTHER. HOW ABOUT *THAT?*"

I was very puzzled. I thought they would probably like each other, Louise's mother and mine. They could talk about babies. They could even talk about Louise and me, if they wanted to; we wouldn't mind. Tatie could serve them tea in the thin cups decorated with blue flowers. Mrs. Donohue liked pretty things; she had a whole collection of cups on a shelf in the dining room, although some had been broken recently when one of the cats, chasing another, had leapt at the shelf.

She eased off her loudness, put her arm around me, and explained, "I don't think your mama would remember me. And I have to stay here to take care of Ralphie and Frankie, same as your mama has to stay home with her baby. But thank you for inviting me, anyway."

And she was right. Mama didn't remember her, though when I told her the name of Louise's mother,

her name before she was married—Peggy O'Reilly—Mama wrinkled her forehead and said finally, "There was a woman named O'Reilly who used to come to our house to do the laundry, and sometimes she brought a little girl. I always wanted to play with that little girl, but she was so shy, as if she were embarrassed to be there. She would never talk to me. I never even knew her name. But maybe it was Peggy."

But I thought that it couldn't have been. It may have been true that the little girl had been embarrassed; but if the little girl had been Peggy O'Reilly, she would have marched right up to my mother, despite the embarrassment, would have admired the yellow dress, and would have bellowed, "HEY. HOW ABOUT THAT!"

I thought often about Louise, her family, and her house, and why I felt so happy with them there. I thought about Charles, his mother, and Tatie, and wondered about their house, to which I had never been permitted to go. I decided that we were all like Jessica's paper dolls: placed neatly in our separate sections in a pleated file. Labeled. I pretended—wished, dreamed—that someday a giant hand would tip the file box upside down, scatter us all from our slots, onto the floor, mixing us together so completely that none of us would know, in the end, who we were, where we belonged, or whether, after all, it even mattered.

W<small>E WENT TO</small> the great-aunts' house for Thanksgiving dinner, Jessica and I dressed alike in pink hand-smocked dresses under our navy blue brass-buttoned coats. We argued about who would push Gordon's enormous English carriage and compromised, each of us walking with one hand on the high handle. Gordon, bundled in a pale blue snowsuit and propped on pillows, grinned toothlessly at us as we bumped and jiggled him along the brick sidewalk of Autumn Street. Mama walked behind us, with Grandmother.

I counted to myself. Three great-aunts, Grandmother, Mama, Jessica, and I.

"There will be seven girls at Thanksgiving dinner," I told Jess, "and only one boy, and he doesn't even count, because he can't eat real food yet."

"I wish Daddy could come," said Jess.

"I wish Grandfather could come," I said.

"Daddy used to give me the wishbone."

"You?" I didn't remember. "Didn't he ever give it to me?"

"No," said Jessica firmly, but I thought she was lying. "He always gave it to me, because you were too little."

There was no way to argue with her, because my memories were gone. "He would give it to me now, though. I'm not too little now."

Jess shrugged.

"Anyway, today maybe the aunts will give it to both of us. What would you wish?"

"I'm not going to *tell*. If you tell wishes they won't come true."

I thought, glumly, that none of my wishes would come true anyway, whether I told them or not. I would wish to be older. To be braver. To be prettier. I would wish that . . .

The baby carriage bumped on a piece of sidewalk distorted by elm roots, and the baby giggled.

We eased the carriage up over the bump, and I finished my thought, almost frightened by it. I would wish that Charles would marry me.

When we were grown up, of course.

*

Great-aunt Caroline, Great-aunt Florence, and Great-aunt Philippa swooped upon us at the doorway with soft cries of greeting, hugs for me and Jess, and expressions of amazement at how Gordon had grown. They passed him back and forth, holding him delicately like a piece of china, until his chin puckered with fear, and Mama smiled and took him back. I could tell that the great-aunts had never held many babies.

They weren't wearing their fluttery summer dresses now, in November. Now the great-aunts were dressed in velvet, deep shades of gray and blue and green, like a trio of expensive dolls, and they each had pearls around their necks. The house was warm and smelled of turkey, of pumpkin and cranberry, piecrusts and breads. We sat in the living room; the grownups talked, Jessica leafed through a magazine, and I watched them all as if I were looking at a painting in a book.

Two little girls in pink dresses. Three elderly ladies in velvet, their hands moving as they talked, their pearls gleaming at their throats. Another elderly lady, sitting stiffly, her neck unadorned, her hands motion-less, her ankles neatly crossed. One woman sitting quietly, holding a baby now asleep against her arm, her head turned toward the little girls, smiling at them.

My mother is beautiful, I thought, for the first time.

The two little girls are sisters. The three ladies in velvet dresses are sisters. Mama is no one's sister. And Grandmother? Did Grandmother have a sister some-where?

What did "aunt" mean? It had something, I knew, to do with sisters. Could it be that *Grandmother* was the sister of the great-aunts?

Relationships were so complicated. But suddenly I had figured one out for myself. I sat up straighter, looked at Grandmother carefully, saw that her eyes were blue, as the great-aunts' were, and that her hair was the same gray as theirs.

"I just figured it out!" I cried in delight. "Grand-mother is your sister!" I looked at the three great-aunts as if they were pieces of a puzzle that I had finally fitted into place.

But there was an awkward silence. Great-aunt Caroline rose to pass the little crystal dish of nuts again.

"No, Elizabeth," said Great-aunt Florence softly, with a smile. "Certainly we do *think* of your grand-mother as a sister . . ."

The other two great-aunts nodded, their heads like birds, smiling, murmuring that it was true, they certainly thought of Grandmother as a sister. Even Grandmother was nodding and murmuring yes, that was true, yes, yes indeed.

Mama laid the baby gently on the couch and told me that she would take me to wash my hands.

"My hands aren't dirty," I whispered to Mama in the hall. "I took a bath just before I came here."

But she took me to the bathroom and closed the door.

"Liz," she said, "it wasn't your fault, because you didn't know. But the aunts were my *real* mother's sisters. So we shouldn't talk about that in front of Grandmother. It might make her feel bad."

"Oh," I said, though I didn't really understand. Dutifully I began to wash my hands.

"Mama, when your mother died, then your father didn't have a wife."

Mama nodded.

"But there were her three sisters. He could have married one of them!" It seemed a lovely thought.

Mama looked uncomfortable. She handed me a thick blue towel and didn't say anything.

"Why didn't he?"

"Goodness, Liz," said Mama. "He fell in love with Grandmother. And that's why people get married."

"Yes, I know," I said sadly. "Except poor Great-aunt Philippa. She fell in love with someone, Tatie told me, but they never got married, and now she just wears that diamond ring to remind herself about it. Probably it makes her very sad."

Mama suddenly looked *very* uncomfortable. "Tatie shouldn't have told you that," she said.

Then I knew. I knew it the same way I had finally known about the sky: that it was all over, not just at the top. I knew it from *seeing* it there, all around me, although no one had ever spoken of it.

"Mama," I said, awed at what I had realized. "Great-aunt Philippa was going to marry *Grandfather,* wasn't she?"

Mama rubbed my dry hands again and again with the blue towel.

"Elizabeth," she said, "you're old enough to know how important it is to keep secrets. I don't want you to say anything about this to *anyone.* Do you understand?"

"But it's true, isn't it, what I said?"

"Yes. It's true. But if you talk about it, it will hurt people. It will hurt Grandmother, and Grandfather, and the aunts."

"I won't even tell Jess."

"All right then."

"Mama, I'll tell you a secret, too."

"What's that, Liz?"

"I know all about falling in love with someone. Because guess what: I'm in love with Charles!" There was a kind of rapture, standing in the small, immaculate bathroom beside my mother, smelling her perfume, feeling the slippery, perfect oval of pale blue soap, and then the rough texture of the thick towel, talking about secret things.

She hugged me. "Just remember, Liz, that sometimes those things don't work out the way you want them to. But it's nice to feel that way, to love someone."

"Yes," I said. "Probably Great-aunt Philippa still feels that way about Grandfather."

"Maybe."

There was a knock at the bathroom door. Jessica called, "It's time! It's time for the turkey!"

At the table I felt supremely happy. I watched Jess, chattering, tossing her curls, and was glad that I knew something that she might never know. I watched my mother, bending toward me to cut my meat, and felt that she had powers of strength and of understanding that I had not before known. I watched my velvet-dressed great-aunt with the sparkling diamond on her hand, laughing softly as she served the vegetables, and was glad that she had loved someone once; and I hoped that for a while—for a little while, at least—he had loved her back.

ALTHOUGH HIS MOUTH remained the damp, cavernous, misshapen puzzle-piece it had been since his stroke in August, I could tell from his eyes that Grandfather remembered Christmas. Tatie and Mama grasped each other's wrists to make a seat of their hands and carried him down the staircase to the library where we were decorating a tree. Grandmother hovered and fluttered like a distraught sparrow until he was arranged in a chair; she tucked a plaid blanket around his thin, pajamaed knees and patted him into a kind of fragile symmetry like a bouquet of dried grass. He made a moist, clicking sound with his mouth.

Click.

Click.

"Why does Grandfather make that sound?" I whispered to Mama, as she unwrapped the carved ornaments from the tissue paper in which they had been packed.

"It's his false teeth," she whispered back.

How terrible to have false teeth. My own two bottom front teeth had fallen out a few months earlier, but bigger new ones had grown in their place. Charles' front top teeth were missing, and he could whistle through the gap and spit great distances; I pushed at my own top ones from time to time with my tongue, but they were recalcitrant and firm. I envied Charles' interstitial grin, but the watery clicks from Grandfather's mouth were unnerving. I scuttled across the rug to his feet and leaned against his covered legs, stroking them as a comfort and apology for his infirmities; it was then, looking up past the clicking mouth into his eyes, that I could tell he remembered Christmas. He was watching the tree intently as Jessica and my mother hung the decorations, and the silvery reflections in the murky mirrors of his face spoke of recollection. I reminded myself to ask Mama later about Christmases when she was a little girl.

Tatie appeared in the doorway, acknowledged the

magnificence of the tree with an awed smile, but spoke to Grandmother dourly.

"Ferdie Gossett's at the back door, ma'am, for his Christmas."

Grandmother rose, said to Mama, "Watch your father, Celia," and followed Tatie to the kitchen. I scampered behind them. *Ferdie Gossett.* I had seen him only from an apprehensive distance before. Now he was right here, in the kitchen, and I wouldn't have missed it for anything, even though it meant leaving the ritual of the tree-trimming and the frail warmth of my grandfather's meager knees.

"Every town has a Ferdie Gossett," my mother had said to me casually when I described to her the man who stood and stared with vacant eyes at the edge of the asphalt playground, during recesses. "He's harmless. But stay away from him."

"What's wrong with him?"

She shook her head. "He was injured somehow."

"In the war?"

"I don't think so. The first war was too long ago. And this war—well, this war is too new, still. He's been around here for several years, since before this war."

"His eyes are funny. Was he injured in his eyes?"

"Oh, Liz. I don't know. It was in his head, I imagine."

"I didn't know there was another war. I thought this was the only one."

Mama had sighed. "There are always wars," she said.

There are always wars; and every town has a Ferdie Gossett. The generalizations were hard for me to comprehend. But the details of the silent presence at the edge of the playground fascinated me. "Where does he live?" I asked her. "Does he have a wife? Children? Why does he wear those terrible clothes?"

"I don't know, Liz. I don't know. Just ignore him."

Now he was in Grandmother's kitchen: for his Christmas, Tatie had said.

And it was true. He sat there, at the kitchen table, his encrusted overcoat pinned closed with a large safety pin, his rheumy eyes peering through the steam of Tatie's soup in a bowl before him. It rolled in narrow streams from the corners of his mouth as he ate. On the floor, leading from the back door, was a track of small dead leaves and mud. Snow was late coming to Pennsylvania; it was gray and cold outside, but the ground was still bare. It had been raining all afternoon. There was dampness in Ferdie Gossett's long fringe of matted hair.

Grandmother moved briskly to the table, unsnapping her purse. She laid a ten-dollar bill on the oilcloth near Ferdie Gossett's bowl.

"We wish you and yours a happy holiday season, Mr. Gossett," she said, matter-of-factly.

He belched. He rubbed his mouth with the sleeve of his filthy coat.

"Tatie," said Grandmother, "be sure to clean everything thoroughly after Mr. Gossett has gone."

I was embarrassed by that. No need, I thought, to point out to Ferdie Gossett that his hygiene was questionable.

Tatie was angry. Not at Grandmother, not at me, but at Ferdie Gossett. "I don't know why we got to put up with this every year," she muttered.

"Do unto others as you would have them do unto you," pronounced Grandmother. "Especially at Christmas. Doesn't the Full Gospel Church teach charity, Tatie?"

"It teach cleanliness," Tatie said darkly, wiping a counter top clear of nonexistent dirt, "and hard work if you wants to eat."

Ferdie Gossett belched again and sucked something away from an upper tooth, noisily.

"Excuse *you*," I said primly, incongruously. It was what Mama said to Gordon when she patted his back after his bottle.

"Merry Christmas to you, Mr. Gossett," said Grandmother. "We will see you again next year. Come along, Elizabeth Jane."

He didn't look up. I noticed his long ragged finger-nails as he snatched up the money, crumpling it into a pocket of his coat. His melancholy, lunatic eyes darted quickly around the kitchen as he stood up and shuffled toward the door. Tatie already held the mop in her hand.

"He didn't even say thank you," I pointed out to Grandmother as we returned to the library.

"He is a tasteless, impolite, and demented man," she replied.

"Then why do you give him money?"

"Because it is Christmas, and I am a Christian."

I sighed, knowing that her gifts to me would be undershirts, a prayer book, and a manicure set in a leather case. I had already opened them, sneaking under the untrimmed tree when everyone was in another part of the house, and rewrapped them carefully. I would have to say thank you, with feigned enthusiasm, to Grandmother on Christmas morning.

"Look, Grandmother! The star!"

While she and I had been in the kitchen dispensing Christian charity and vegetable soup to Ferdie Gossett, Mama had balanced on a chair to put the golden star in place at the top of the tree. For a moment, my resentment at the undershirts and prayer book faded; I stood in the center of the room, looking up, and saw the star reflect everything: the tall bookcases filled with leather-bound volumes in orderly rows; the deep red and blue patterns of the Oriental rug; the brightly colored packages heaped on the floor; my sister, her blonde hair shining; and the plaid cocoon that held the pale fluttery moths of my grandfather's hands.

Click.

Click.

I sank again to the floor beside him, happy and safe, and made the same sound with my own tongue against my teeth. His head bobbed in a benedictory gesture. His teeth clicked. I smiled at him, rubbed my cheek against his fingers, and tried to echo the small noise: click, click. We looked at the star, the tree, the comforting room filled with Christmas; and we made the sound to each other, a tiny staccato duet, as if we were traveling together on tiptoe to places where neither of us had yet been.

*

Mama gave me paints for Christmas—paints and an easel—and although the sky outside was still a December sky, as gray as the undershirt exposed at Ferdie Gosset's grizzled throat and as forbidding as his murky eyes, I made my own skies once again. Grandmother said that I could not paint in my room. She wanted no splatters, she said, on the hand-hooked rug.

But Tatie made space in the laundry room and helped me stand my easel there. She gave me an old shirt. It had been my grandfather's, but the once-firm lines of his shoulders were no longer outlined there. It fell in soft folds around me, and I put a deliberate daub of blue on the pocket with a flourish. Then I dipped the wide camel-hair brush in blue again and swept it across the paper to create a world of sunshine, summer, and space.

When I added yellow to my green, I found that I had made the color of the Pennsylvania countryside beyond our small town. Behind the meadows I painted the deep blue-green shadowy woods.

"Sweet heaven, that's just beautiful," said Tatie, and thumbtacked the painting to the laundry room wall.

Lillian Chestnut came into the laundry room with an armload of sheets.

"I'm not going to be in your way, Lillian," I said, forestalling her objections. "Tatie said that if I stay right in this corner I won't be in your way."

But she was looking at my painting with a smile.

"I used to live on a farm," she said. She put the sheets on the floor in a heap, leaned against the washing machine, and lit a cigarette.

"What was it like?"

"Pretty. All green like that picture." Then she laughed shortly. "Hard work, though. Eleven children in my family."

"*Eleven!* Tell me their names."

"Oh, lord, let me think. Alfred, he was the oldest, then Patsy, and Florence. Jakie. Ben. Then me. After me, Norman and Cal, they're twins. And then Jean, and Ruth, and the youngest is Shirley."

"Which one do you like best?"

"Jakie," she said, without hesitating.

"Why?"

Lillian shrugged. "He was just the nicest. He taught me to drive a car. He has yellow hair, like yours."

"Where is he now? Back on the farm, driving a tractor? Do you ever see him?"

"No, he's in the Navy someplace. Jakie and Ben and Norman and Cal, they're all in the Navy."

"At the war, like Daddy?"

"Yeah."

I sighed. "*Everybody's* at the war. Who takes care of your farm, now that everybody's at the war?"

"My father and my brother Alfred."

"Do you miss it? The farm?"

Lillian laughed. "No. Farms aren't any fun." She looked at the painting again. "Sometimes it was pretty, though. In the spring it was pretty."

"I bet you miss Jakie, though, because you liked him best."

"Yeah. I miss Jakie some."

She hissed water from the laundry sink over the end of her cigarette and threw it into the wastebasket. She leaned over to sort the sheets.

"Mama doesn't like any one of us best. I asked her who she liked best, and she said she loved us each the same amount."

"Yeah? Well, I guess mothers are like that. Or else they don't tell who they like best."

"Who do you like best, of me and Jess? You don't have to count Gordon, because you don't really know him."

"You."

I had known she would say it, or I wouldn't have dared to ask the question. Old Roasted Chestnut. For a moment I loved her.

"If you want," I told her shyly, "you can have the painting when it dries, and hang it in your room. You don't have to if you don't want to."

She closed the lid of the washing machine, added soap through the special opening, and turned it on. She looked at the painting for a long time; and then Lillian, too, became shy.

"Do you think maybe you could make a different one for me?" she asked. "With the sky and the field and all. But then out in the middle of the field, right there," she pointed, "could you maybe paint a tractor, and put a guy with yellow hair sitting on it?"

"Jakie?"

"Yeah. And make him sort of looking off there toward the woods? Like he had stopped the tractor to rest, and was just sitting there thinking?"

I could see Jakie in my mind. For the tractor I would have to find a picture in *Life* magazine or the *Saturday Evening Post,* to try to copy. It wouldn't be easy. But I could see Jakie in my mind.

"Sure. I'll do it after lunch, and it can be your Christmas present, because I didn't give you one."

"Thanks."

Lillian began to take the clean, dry socks from a wooden rack and to sort them into pairs. Mine and Jessica's: she matched them and rolled them neatly into bright-colored balls. I could hear Tatie putting plates around the dining room table, and knew that it was time for lunch.

"Lillian?"

"Yeah?"

"I hope he comes back safe from the war. Jakie, I mean."

She matched the toes of two red knee socks and smoothed them with her hand.

"Yeah," she said. "Well, maybe he will, maybe he won't."

She shrugged: that nonchalant, I-don't-care gesture that she made with her shoulders, often. I was puzzled.

She loved Jakie, I could tell; why, then, would she lift her shoulders that way, as if it didn't matter whether he came back safe?

Then, because I saw that Lillian's mouth was set stiffly, unlike her everyday face, I knew. I understood. It was a disguise, a mask not unlike the one I had worn at Halloween, when I had been taken outdoors after dark to an Autumn Street filled with what had seemed perilous horrors; and in covering my face I had hidden my fear.

It was all a kind of pretending. It explained why Great-aunt Philippa, whatever her private feelings were, could flutter her hand with its years-old diamond ring, could say that she thought of Grandmother as a sister, and could smile. It was why Mama said "Don't worry" off-handedly when we asked about Daddy, even if she had had no letters in a very long time. It was why Grandmother, often now, acted as if everything were still the same, as if Grandfather hadn't changed, as if the wheelchair meant nothing at all. It was why Tatie sometimes turned her broad back, offering no protection, no consolation, when I had been scolded and came to her, sobbing, for solace. And it was what had compelled me once, to my shame, to call Charles "nigger."

It was a kind of pretending composed of pride, of

the pain of powerlessness, of need—and fear of need—
and it came from caring: from caring so much that you
were fearful for your own self, and how alone you
were, or might someday be.

My THROAT HURT. But I didn't tell Mama. I swallowed the coughs that started deep in my chest. Mama would have rubbed me with camphorated oil, covered my ribs with a cut square of flannel, and put me to bed. I would have missed playing with Charles, who was coming for the weekend.

Valentine's Day was past. But in my room, in my bureau drawer under my neatly rolled socks, I had saved the special Valentine I had made for Charles. It was red construction paper, stolen from school, and a lace paper doily pasted neatly on the front. Inside, in my best printing, it said, "Be mine."

I wondered if there had been a Valentine mailbox at Charles' school, and if there were girls in his first grade who had asked him to be theirs.

If so, it didn't matter because I had something else to offer him. I had a new, unused sled, and there was fresh snow in the park across the street, where the smoothest hills in town could be found.

"Did you bring your boots, Charles?" I asked him, when I found him in the kitchen with Tatie late Saturday morning.

"Of course I brung my boots. You think I want to ruin these good school shoes?" Charles held up his feet, proud of a brand new pair of brown leather shoes with plaid laces.

"Those are nice."

"Yeah, they ain't so bad." He was shy, suddenly, and tucked his feet around the rung of the kitchen chair.

"Tatie, you know what I want? Hot lemonade with honey in it."

"You got a sore throat, Elizabeth?" asked Tatie suspiciously.

"No," I lied. My throat was like sandpaper. "I just thought maybe Charles would like some. Would you, Charles?"

"Yeah, that sound pretty good."

Tatie gave it to us, steaming, in thick mugs. We sat together at the kitchen table and sipped.

"Guess what, Charles. I got a new sled."

"Yeah? What kind?"

"Flexible Flyer."

"Little or big?"

"A big one. You want to go sledding with me?"

"Where?" Charles looked glumly into his mug, and then sideways at Tatie, who was at the stove, starting some soup.

"Across the street."

Charles sighed and kicked his chair with his new shoes. "I can't. I ain't allowed to go in front."

"That ain't in front. It's . . ."

Tatie looked at me sternly. "Don't say 'ain't,' Elizabeth."

I sighed. "It isn't in front. It isn't in the front yard, and it isn't on the sidewalk. It's way way across the street, through the park. He can go there, Tatie, can't he? Let him, Tatie. I've been saving my sled all this time so that Charles could go with me."

Tatie stirred her soup and turned the gas flame to low. She thought. Finally she said, "All right. Charles can go. But you go out the back door, and pull your sled up the side street over to the park. You got mittens, Charles?"

"Yeah. The red ones Mrs. Wiltsie give me for Christmas."

"You sure you don't have a sore throat, Elizabeth?"

"I'm sure," I lied again. I ran to the front hall closet to get my snowsuit and my boots.

"Mama," I called up the stairs. "I'm going sledding."

She came to the top of the landing. "Well," she said, laughing. "I was beginning to think you were never going to try out that new sled. It's cold out, though. You have Tatie help you with your snowsuit, and be sure to wear your warmest mittens, and . . ."

"I will, Mama," I said impatiently.

"And, Liz . . ."

"What?"

"Remember what I told you about the sled. You be careful."

"I will. I promise."

Outside, Charles and I pretended we were smoking Lucky Strikes, blowing our steamy breath into the gray, cold day. I flung myself into the fresh backyard snow and made an angel, dragging my arms into wings. Charles made an angel beside mine.

"Twin angels. When Grandfather's on the upstairs porch he can look down and see them," I told Charles.

"They not twins. Mine bigger than yours."

"Not much. Only a little." But Charles was right. During the winter he had become taller than I. "I'm going to be seven next month. Then I'll catch up with you."

"Maybe."

We walked across the park, each of us holding part of the sled's rope, pulling it behind us. It ran smoothly across the snow with the thin quick sound of a knife-blade.

"Know what Mama told me about sleds?"

"What?"

"If you touch your tongue to the runner, it will freeze there. Your tongue will be stuck to the sled."

"Why you wanna put your tongue there?"

"I don't know. But some people do, and then their tongue is stuck there forever."

"Hoooie. How they get it off?"

"I don't know. I suppose they have to cut off your tongue."

"Or else leave it there, and then you got a sled on you for the rest of your life."

We both thought about that. It was terrifying.

"How would you eat, I wonder?"

"Spoon it in under the sled. Plunk your sled onto the table when it's eating time, and spoon the old food right in under."

I swallowed, thinking about it. The back of my tongue felt like a raw wound. I picked up a handful of snow and ate it, savoring the cold on my sore throat.

"You not supposed to eat snow. It's poison."

"Is not. I eat it all the time."

"Well, dogs pee on it. You just ate dog pee, probably."

"Liar. I picked a clean white place."

"You wanna know something dirty?" Charles lowered his voice.

"Sure."

"If you pee outside in winter, it freeze right in the air. Freeze right into a big sticking-out icicle."

"*Really?* How do you know? Did you do it?"

"Of course I didn't do it, stupid. You think I want a icicle sticking outa my pants? I just know, is all. Somebody told me."

"Look. There's the hill."

"Hoooie!"

Charles and I ran with the sled toward the top of the Autumn Park hill. I would have been frightened without him. There were other children there, bigger ones, mostly boys. The kind of children who scared me, with their loud, boisterous voices; old enough that they no longer wore snowsuits with thick, baggy leggings. Their corduroy pants were wet and crusty wtih ice, and they were flinging themselves onto their sleds, yelling, and speeding down the hill, steering dangerously close to the rocks at the bottom.

"We could find a smaller hill," I said nervously to Charles.

"No, this one the best one," he said, but he said it uncertainly. We trudged closer to the top of the hill. I recognized some of the boys there from school. Sixth graders. Eugene Shields. Tommy Rasmussen, who had pushed me on the playground once. Johnny Mc-Kittrick, with his thick red hair sticking out from under a knitted cap. I was petrified of them all.

"What do you guys want?" one of them said suddenly, looking at Charles and me.

"We're going sledding," I answered him, but I knew my voice was so soft that it could barely be heard. "We're going to try out my new sled," I said, a little louder.

"Who's he?" asked Johnny McKittrick, standing so close to me that I could see the viscid stream from his runny nose. He was looking at Charles, who was silent.

"He's my friend. His name is Charles."

"He can't come here. He can't sled on this hill."

"Why not?"

But Johnny McKittrick didn't answer. He licked at the drippings from his nose and reached toward the rope of my sled. "Lemme see your sled."

Hold on to it, Charles, I thought. Don't let go. But Charles' mittened hand unclenched, and he released the rope. So did I. Johnny McKittrick took my sled.

"You can try it once," I said anxiously. "But then give it back."

One of the other boys leaned down suddenly, collected a mitten full of dirty snow, and lunged forward to smear it in Charles' face.

"Don't!" I cried. But Charles still was voiceless, standing stiffly as if he were frozen there at the top of the Autumn Park Hill. The snow was sliding on his face, down into the collar of his coat.

"Do something, Charles!" I said to him fiercely. But he was stricken, silent, and helpless. The big boys had turned from us and taken my sled with them to the starting-off place. Johnny McKittrick looked back and called, "We'll give it back when we're finished with it. But get him off this hill."

They piled, three of them, in layers, onto my new sled and sailed, whooping, down the packed snow, smaller and smaller, as I watched helplessly. When I turned back to Charles, he was gone; I saw him with his back to me, trudging through the snow, not toward Grandfather's house, but heading toward the upper end of the park, toward the end of Autumn Street.

When I caught up with him, I could see that he was crying, and I had never seen Charles cry before.

"Is your face okay? Did they hurt you?"

"Shut up."

"They'll give the sled back."

"I don't care about your ole sled."

I plodded beside him through the deep, untrammeled snow. It worked its way into the tops of my boots and down inside my socks so that my feet began to feel as wounded as my raw throat. My whole body ached with cold. And inside me somewhere I ached with something else, something that had nothing to do with my sled, but was connected with Charles' tears. I searched for redemptive things to say to him.

"If you cry outside in winter, maybe you'll get icicles on your face."

He turned on me furiously and pushed me down. I fell into the thick, stinging snow, and it coated my neck and wrists. I lost a mitten. Charles stopped and stood over me, angry, as I floundered, trying to get up. Finally he gave me his hand. I took it, and tried to find a way to cheer him.

"Charles," I said when I was upright, shivering, "do you want to go into the woods?"

"I'm goin' into the woods and I'm goin' to find me a cave, and you ain't comin'," he said.

"Let me come."

"You jest a baby."

"No, I'm not. I won't be scared."

"You scared of them turtles."

"Not with you, I won't be."

168

"Promise?"

"I promise."

It was a lie, and I knew that it was. But I took his hand, trying to warm my bare one against his wet red mitten, and went with him to the woods at the end of Autumn Street. Far behind us, the shouts of the boys who had my sled grew fainter until we heard nothing at all as we entered the dark woods by the path on which only a few footprints showed. It began to snow again, silently covering those, and our own.

There had been no sun all day; and now, with the new snow, the grayness of the morning's sky blurred so that the whole world was a gray-white mass, bitter cold, and darkened by the heavy overhanging pines that bordered the narrow path. It was absolutely soundless: none of the chattering squirrels and noisy birds of summer, and even our own steps were as mute as the tread of ghosts, through the new powder of the freshly falling snow.

"Where them caves?" demanded Charles. We were barely into the woods. I could still see, even through the snowfall, the outline of Autumn Street.

"I don't know." My voice was raspy and my throat so filled with pain that it was almost unbearable to speak.

"Well, where them turtles, then?"

"Charles, I don't feel good." My head was suddenly

spinning inside, as if the knives in my throat had cut loose whatever held my thoughts in place.

"WHERE THEM TURTLES?"

And I knew, despite the lurching emptiness in my head, what I had probably always known. I sank to my knees on the snowy path, unable to hold myself up anymore. I started to cry.

"Charles, there aren't any turtles."

"Liar."

Did he mean that I was a liar for having told him, long ago, that there were? Or for saying, now, that there were not? I didn't know. It didn't matter. There was something wrong with our being in the woods at all, something far more frightening than turtles or caves, and the certainty of that fluttered in my head like a bat, clawing at me, but I couldn't keep it still to think about it, to exorcise it, or to explain.

"Charles," I whimpered. "I'm sick. Something's the matter with me. Take me home."

"Go home yourself. I'm stayin'."

"Please come with me."

I looked up at him and saw him shake his head firmly. He wouldn't come. I stood up, swaying with dizziness, and pulled at his arm, partly to support myself, partly as a plea. But he turned his back. Finally I willed my numb feet to move, back along the path, toward the street, through the place where our foot-prints had been layered over and lost.

*

I left him there. I left him there alone, because he wouldn't come, and because my head swam with fever and the terrifying knowledge that one can, after all, save only oneself.

It was true, what I told him, that there were no turtles in the woods, and I knew it then. But there was some other danger there, and we both knew that; we could feel it in the snow and the silence, as small as we were. With the hot knives in my throat and the buzzing pain that had begun to be a sharp-toothed creature in my head, I had none of the strength or courage to stay and face the danger with him, and none left of the anger that made him stay there alone.

He was taller than I was, it was true. The angels that we had made together in Grandfather's yard had shown it. But he was so little. I looked back at him, standing there resolutely on the curving, overhung path, his dark face proud and defiant, his red Christmas mittens bright through the swirling snow, and I knew how little we both were. But my head was spinning and hot, and my vision was beginning to blur from sickness, the relentless snow, and my own tears.

"Please come," I said once more, and perhaps he

heard me; but he had already turned away to go farther, deeper, into the woods. I stumbled, crying, all the way home; and the street, changed by the snowfall and the distortions of beginning delirium, was endless and unfamiliar.

When I reached Grandfather's kitchen, Tatie's soup was still simmering on the stove, the same soup she had been starting when we left. So no more than an hour or two had passed. But time had stopped for me. It could have been days, or years, or a lifetime, since I had trudged away with Charles and the sled.

"I don't feel good," I cried, and Tatie stripped my sodden, ice-filled clothes from me as I stood shaking on the kitchen floor. "And Charles wouldn't come back. He's in the woods at the end of Autumn Street."

"That Charles." Tatie peeled me down to my underwear and rubbed my arms and legs briskly with her warm hands. "Don't you worry none about him. You're catching a cold, child. Your voice sound like bullfrogs. You run up and get yourself in a nice hot bath. Charles, he be back when he's ready. He gets stubborn, sometimes."

But the bath didn't help. I lay in the hot water shivering, and finally, half-dry and naked, I climbed into my bed, something I had never voluntarily done in the mid-afternoon.

My mother came in. "You've missed lunch, Liz.

Tatie says you're catching a cold. Do you want her to bring some soup up to you?"

I shook my head, the covers drawn up tight around my neck. "I just want to sleep. I'm so tired, Mama. It was so cold out."

She touched my forehead, and her hand felt cool. "You have a fever. If you're not better later this afternoon I'll call the doctor."

"Mama?" I was already half-asleep, my thoughts dissolving into the heat inside my head.

"What, sweetie?"

"Charles is up in the woods. He wouldn't come back with me."

"Did you tell Tatie?"

"I think so." I couldn't remember.

"Well, don't worry. Charles can find his way home, and he'll come back when he gets cold."

She went away, and I let the heat melt all my thoughts, and I slept.

It was almost dark, the early dark of winter, when I woke, coughing and confused, and remembered Charles again. I climbed from the bed, pulled on my flannel nightgown, and walked groggily into the upstairs hall, touching the wallpaper to keep my balance. Mama was coming up the stairs. I wanted to tell her that my throat felt like hot splinters.

"Elizabeth, it's getting dark, and Charles hasn't come

back. Tatie's very worried. We all are. Tell us exactly where you left him."

I sat on the top step, pulled my nightgown around me for warmth, and told her.

"We went into the woods at the end of Autumn Street. And I got scared, and didn't feel good, so I wanted to come home. But Charles wouldn't come. When I left him he was on the path that goes into the woods, near the place where you can see the big rock from the road."

She nodded and left me there. I sat, shivering, swallowing again and again, testing the pain in my throat, and listened to people talking downstairs, in low voices. The voices swam into my head, back and forth, in slow motion, and through my fever I couldn't sort them out. Mama's voice. Tatie's. The clock striking. And soon, men's voices in the front hall. The sounds of boots stamping off snow, doing it right on the front hall rug, something Grandmother never permitted. I sat still, my head against the wall, and half-slept, half-listened. Full darkness came; lights were turned on, downstairs, but I huddled in shadows at the top of the stairs, shaking and drifting in and out of sleep and the beginnings of interrupted dreams.

Police came. I thought that was a dream. But I startled myself awake and listened. There were police downstairs, stamping snow off, and Mama's voice.

Tatie's, saying Charles' name. There was fear. Worried sounds. And outside, there was darkness. Darkness and snow.

The dreams began coming again, in bright colors that carved pain in my head, and I was not sure if I was awake or asleep. I forgot Charles, forgot the police and the snow, remembered only the way to my bed, and felt my way there where it would be warmer, safer. I slept again.

There were nightmares, which seemed to go on forever, from which I woke again and again in the dark with a feeling of fear that transferred itself on waking into the pain that now lodged deep in my chest. Again and again I sat up suddenly in my bed, to find night still there, to hear voices still downstairs, and to slide back into sleep.

Then the real nightmare came, as light came back with the beginning of morning, and the real nightmare was not part of my sleep. It was the men's voices again, the stamping of snow again, so much noise that I once more climbed from bed and felt my way to the top of the stairs, and heard that Charles was dead.

In the woods. In the woods. I heard them say that, and I heard Tatie's low cry. I had known that the danger was in the woods. Charles had known. We hadn't understood the form of the danger, had imagined it to be turtles, caves, or even the red-headed boy who licked lustily at the dripping from his own nose. But it was none of those. I staggered down the stairs to the place where the lights were on; they didn't hear me come in my bare, cold, quiet feet. Perhaps if they had seen me they would not have said in my presence, for I was still only six, that Charles had been killed by the half-mad derelict who wandered through the streets of Grandfather's town. Charles had been killed when he had come upon Ferdie Gossett in the woods at the end of Autumn Street.

I stood at the foot of the stairs, unseen, and heard them speak of it, the most unspeakable of things, in my grandfather's house, while upstairs my grandfather slept with his speechless dreams, his powers of protection gone. In my own anguished delirium I could see Charles, so small; and I could see the man into whose furtive-eyed face I had sometimes glanced with timid curiosity as he stood alone, a victim himself. With their different angers, their different terms of innocence, the two had met in the woods that I had always feared for the wrong reasons. And the man had carried with him a knife. He had cut Charles' throat from one side to the other. When I heard the policeman say that, I heard the clean whisper of a sled runner slice through packed snow, and I cried out and fell.

It was Tatie who picked me up and held me close in her massive, inviolate arms. I remember that. I remember that her low moans filled the high-ceilinged hallway, that she clasped me against her, nearly crushing me as if to crush my pain and hers, as if to ward off more. She murmured unintelligible words to me, rocking me against her; and the words became wails, high-pitched chants, almost songs, almost magic: they were wails I had never heard before, wails not part of my own heritage or understanding. But they blurred and softened the edges of my terror.

The others stood motionless, silent, and watched. Her sounds were a litany for which, in the dim early morning winter light of the high-ceilinged hallway, there was no response.

Finally she lifted her head. Her body was shuddering, still, but her voice, when she spoke, was very firm.

"Call a doctor," she said. "This child's on fire. Let's not lose this one, too."

My mother, her face pale and stricken, moved quickly to the telephone.

For days there was a haze in the room, so that everything was veiled; but the haze seemed to be behind my own eyes, deep in the hot part of my head, where something ached and throbbed with the same rhythm as my pulse.

My whole body was burning. I thrashed and kicked the blankets aside and then shook uncontrollably with chills. Through the haze, someone replaced the blankets again and again, and wiped my face with a damp cloth. From time to time a cool spoon was placed against my mouth; someone held a firm, supporting arm to my back, lifting me, and liquids I couldn't taste were given to me from the spoon. I turned my head from side to side, trying to refuse; it took all my energy to breathe, and I couldn't summon the strength to swallow. Phantoms pressed against my chest. Each breath was pain. I couldn't dislodge the heaviness that gripped my ribs; through the darkness and the haze, I planned each breath, trying to find a way around the weight. Finally, desperate, I would take the breath, gasping, but the weight and pain were always there; and I cried, fighting it, fighting the breathing itself, unable not to breathe, frantic to escape the pain, the heat, and the monstrous things that screamed and raked their claws inside my head.

Sometimes there were bright lights. There was a man who came, who spoke to me, who said, "Elizabeth, Elizabeth," in a deep, demanding voice from which I turned away, and who raised my nightgown gently and then stabbed my shaking bottom with needles.

But mostly there were shadows and darkness and dreams. I could see Charles in the dreams, and I could see him again when my eyes were open, looking at me through the haze; I could see his dark face with the mouth molded into a scream. His mouth was like Grandfather's, open and black; but the eyes were Charles' eyes, little-boy eyes, wide and frightened, not at all like the tired, puzzled stare of an old man.

I could see his neck, red and open as a grin.

I shrieked into the dark room, into the night, into my own dreams, shrieked even through the pain that pulled tighter around my chest. And they came again, people whose names I no longer knew; lights went on, and the cool hands sponged my face one more time, and one more time, and one more time.

Through the haze I could hear my mother cry. It may have been a dream; there was a time when the dreams were as real as the other, when night and day were the same, and when no one's tears mattered but my own.

Then the weight and pain began to lift. Breathing began to happen without thought. I was able, now and then, to focus on things through the lifted haze: my mother's face, swimming into my sight and disappearing again; a glass of water on the table; a picture hanging, as it always had, on my bedroom wall. Everything I had known was the same, and yet it was all different. It all seemed new and flat, without interest. And I was more tired than I had ever been. Too tired to keep my eyes open, but too frightened of my dreams to sleep. I lay stunned and mute, awake, silent, waiting. I let them lift me, wash me, feed me; but my eyes stayed closed while I waited for the next unspeakable thing, not knowing what it would be, or how it would come, but certain that it would happen and that I would not be able to keep it away.

One morning it was my mother's voice that I heard through the secret darkness of my closed eyes. "Elizabeth," she said to me, "it's the first day of spring."

I let her words float, pulsing, through my head, searching for the unwounded place where they would have meaning.

"It's your birthday," she said gently. "You're seven years old today."

And the meaning pierced my consciousness, inside where the sounds had subsided. February was gone. March had come and was almost past. Charles had been seven. Now I was. I turned my head away from Mama's words.

But she touched my shoulders and shook me softly. "I have a surprise for you," she said. "Will you open your eyes to see it?"

I kept my eyes tightly closed and said nothing.

"Your daddy's back," she told me. "Open your eyes now, Elizabeth."

So I did, at last; and the first thing I saw on my seventh birthday was my father. He stood in the doorway, wearing the uniform that I remembered, smiling at me; and I remembered his smile, I remembered his face, I remembered in a rush all the things about my father that I had thought gone forever.

When he walked toward my bed, it was slowly, and I saw that he was leaning on a cane. The sight made

181

me curiously happy; it linked him to my grandfather, redeeming the dignity of the old man who now sat slumped and helpless in the house he had always commanded. Somehow the cane, and my father's slow, uneven steps, gave a continuity to the world and made it seem firm enough to hold me once again.

He sat on my bed and put his arms around me, nuzzling my neck with his nose the way he always had. I held tightly to him.

"Daddy, bad things have happened to me," I whispered, my hands knotted together behind his shoulders so that he could never leave again.

"I know," he whispered back. "But they're all over now. Bad things won't happen any more."

I believed him, when he told me that. I think that he believed it, too.

Bad things had happened to my father, so I knew that he understood. Part of his leg was gone. He had a new lower leg, made of wood and metal in fascinating, complicated combinations. After the first, startling sight of the place where his real leg ended and the new one began, it didn't seem terrible any more. He taught me, while I was still in bed, recovering, to say "prosthesis," and it was only then, when I tried to say it and failed in a wonderful mixture of spit and giggles, that I realized my two front teeth were gone. Sometime during the time of nightmares and pneumonia they had fallen out; so I had continued to grow, and it was true, what my father had said, that the bad things were all over. I was seven and safe.

Gordon, the baby, had grown two new front teeth in exactly the same place where mine were missing, during the month that I was sick. And he could stand by himself, startled and wobbly, for a few seconds before he fell. Jess brought him to my room to show me, and she was kind to me, glad I was well. She had a bedroom of her own now, because I'd been sick; but it was not for that reason that she was kind, I knew.

Grandmother appeared in my doorway now and then, with her stiff face, to inquire how I felt. I answered her politely, but I didn't think she really cared. All of her time was still spent with Grandfather; when she came to my doorway, it was always with his medicine, or the book that she was reading to him, in one hand.

Finally I was allowed to go downstairs alone. I put on my bathrobe and my pink slippers of soft fur and went to visit Tatie in the kitchen. I vowed that I would never speak to her, or anyone, of Charles.

She welcomed me with a hug, oatmeal cookies, and tears that she thought I didn't see in her dark eyes.

"Child," she said, "I was so worried about you."

There was in having been sick a wonderful status that I had never enjoyed before. "Everyone was worried about me," I said proudly.

"Lord, that's true all right. Your mama, she was up nights pacing the floor . . ."

"Really?" I was delighted.

"Really. Course, she was worried about your daddy, too, when he got hisself injured . . ."

"But it was just his leg. Mine was my *whole body* that was sick."

"That's surely true, Elizabeth."

"And Jessica was worried too, I bet."

"My goodness, that Jessica, she up in her room every night, making get-well cards, and then you too sick to look at them, sometimes she cried."

"Oh, yes, Jessica must have been very upset." I savored it all, along with the oatmeal cookies.

"And your grandma . . ."

"Ha," I interrupted. "Grandmother doesn't care about *anybody*, except Grandfather."

There was a silence, and then Tatie turned on me furiously, something she had never done before.

"Don't you speak of your grandma that way, Elizabeth."

"But she doesn't, Tatie. She . . ."

"Let me just tell you something. And then I don't want to talk of it no more, do you understand?"

I nodded.

"Your grandma, on the day that we bury Charles . . ."

"Oh, Tatie, I don't want to talk about that. I really don't."

"Then you just listen. You don't have to do no talking. Your grandma, on that day, she go up to her room and she puts on her black coat and her black hat with them feathers, and she calls her a taxi, and she tells the taxi to take her to the Full Gospel Church.

"Now you don't know this, Elizabeth, 'cause you too little, but in this town there ain't a cab driver that's gonna take a white lady to the Full Gospel without arguing. And I know this happened, because the cab driver, he told Gwendolyn. He told Gwendolyn that he try to talk your grandma out of going to the Full Gospel Church on the day we buried Charles, and your grandma, she put on that mad face she gets sometimes, and she tell that cabbie to shut his mouth and start driving.

"Me, I'm sitting in the Full Gospel sanctuary, already starting my grieving, and the whole church full by then, and in walks your grandma, Elizabeth, in her black feathered hat, and she the only white person in that whole place. Your grandma in her whole life, child, never been the only white person in a room. But she walks right up that aisle and she sees there's a place right near to me, and she sits herself down in it, sitting just as straight as she sits at that dinner table when I'm passing the meal around.

"And when we singing 'Sweet Child Jesus' I looks over at your grandma, sitting right there amidst all the Hallelujahs and the Praise Lords—and they don't have none of those at that church your grandma goes to every Sunday; I know that for a real fact, Elizabeth—and she's sitting there singing the words right out of the book. And there are tears coming down your grandma's cheeks, just the same as there are tears coming down all the colored cheeks in that church, for Charles, and she no more care, right then, what color she is, or I am."

I was watching Tatie, but she wasn't looking at me. She was looking somewhere inside her own head.

"You," she said suddenly, scornfully, "tears come easy to you, Elizabeth. You cry when you get into trouble and get caught. You cry when you stub your toe.

"And me—well, tears come easy to me, too.

"But for your grandma to come to the Full Gospel Church and weep for Charles: that didn't come easy for her. And your mama don't know that she did that. Your daddy don't know it, and your sister don't know it. The only reason I'm telling you is because you got a hateful kind of bigotry for your grandma, and I don't want to hear no more of it."

She was correct, that tears came easily to me. I began to cry then. It was not for my grandmother that I cried, or even for Charles; it was for me and Tatie, and that there was anger between us for the first time.

"I don't have a hateful bigotry, Tatie," I sobbed. "Really, I don't."

"Your grandma don't know how to show her heart is all," Tatie said. "Do you understand that?"

"Yes," I wept. "But I know how. And you do."

She relented, then, and took me into her lap. My legs had grown longer, it seemed, while I was sick; they were in the way, suddenly, outgrowing Tatie, and I sat awkwardly, my backside still bruised and aching from the needles. But my arms felt their familiar way around her wide bosom, and I put my head against her shoulder while I cried. She rocked me back and forth, forgiving me, and through the starched clean cotton of her uniform I could feel the strong and stable rhythm of her heart.

*

It was such a long time ago. Probably my father and I both knew, even then, that it was not true, what we told each other, that bad things would never happen again. But we needed that lie, that pretending, the spring that I was seven. We had both lost so much. He had told me his secret: that sometimes, in the night, he felt a deep, unassuageable pain in the place where his leg had been; and I had whispered to him of mine, of the hollow place inside me where I ached with memory and with fear. We told each other, promised each other, that the pain and the fear would go away. It was not ever to be true. But there are times—times of anguish—when an impossible promise to someone you love is as sweet as a cinnamon-smudged fingertip, as nourishing and necessary as the sunlight that comes, still, to consecrate Autumn Street in summer.